"Garland's sizzling dialogue and brisk pace will whisk readers through the streets of Chicago in this well-crafted mystery. A real page-turner."

—Connie Briscoe, author of *Big Girls Don't Cry*

"Draw[s] readers in with its honest view of the struggles of families and neighborhoods that have been torn apart by drugs and violence. The fast-paced narrative gives readers a feel for the decisions that are made in the newsrooms across America. *DETAILS AT TEN* has both humor and page-turning suspense. This high-powered romantic thriller is one book you won't want to put down."

—*Black Issues Book Review*

"*DETAILS AT TEN* capably asks a question, then gradually answers it with a series of neat plot twists and turns."

—*Chicago Sun-Times*

"Georgia Barnett is a smart, sassy, sexy television reporter who solves baffling crime cases in Chicago. A dynamic new sleuth is on the scene. *DETAILS AT TEN* will capture your attention and your heart."

—Valerie Wilson Wesley, author of the Tamara Hayle mysteries

"*DETAILS AT TEN* offers a vivid cast of characters."

—*St. Petersburg Times* (FL)

"Ardella Garland makes an impressive debut in *DETAILS AT TEN*, which is smart, realistic, and packs a punch. Her television reporter is the perfect sleuth, giving us refreshing new blood in the mystery/suspense genre."

—Tananarive Due, author of *The Living Blood* and *My Soul to Keep*

DETAILS AT 10

YOLANDA JOE

WRITING AS ARDELLA GARLAND

POCKET **STAR** BOOKS
New York   London   Toronto   Sydney   Singapore

This book is a work of fiction. Names, characters, places and incidents are products of the author's imagination or are used fictitiously. Any resemblance to actual events or locales or persons, living or dead, is entirely coincidental.

A Pocket Star Book published by
POCKET BOOKS, a division of Simon & Schuster, Inc.
1230 Avenue of the Americas, New York, NY 10020

Copyright © 2000 by Yolanda Joe

Originally published in hardcover in 2000 by Simon & Schuster, Inc.

ISBN: 0-7434-1480-2

First Pocket Books printing February 2002

10 9 8 7 6 5 4 3 2 1

POCKET STAR BOOKS and colophon are registered trademarks of Simon & Schuster, Inc.

For information regarding special discounts for bulk purchases, please contact Simon & Schuster Special Sales at 1-800-456-6798 or business@simonandschuster.com

Cover photo by Barry Marcus

Printed in the U.S.A.

Acknowledgments

Thanks to . . .

My family and friends who love and encourage me.

My dynamite agent and friend Victoria . . . I create and she makes it happen.

My editor, Constance, for her keen sense of how to shape a story. . . . And Tracy too for being a tireless supporter of this project.

And last, but not least, my writing peers, whose wo⌐ derful novels and poetry inspire me to push myself har⌐ to create new and interesting work.

for
Karen E. Hodge,
a friend and a fighter

DETAILS AT 10

(***PACKAGE***)

Natural sound cop shouting

("Get back, get back . . .")
(**REPORTER TRACK**)

CRIME SCENE: COP/FLASHING LIGHTS/
CROWD
CHYRON LOCATION: SOUTH SIDE

A CHICAGO COP TRIES TO
CONTROL A SMALL CROWD
LURED BY GUNSHOTS AND
SIRENS TO WHAT TURNED OUT
TO BE A GRISLY MURDER SCENE.

PAN FACES IN CROWD/BULLET SHELLS
ON GROUND

THE PEOPLE, YOUNG AND OLD,
PRESSED THEIR BODIES
AGAINST THE YELLOW CRIME
SCENE TAPE. THEY WATCHED AS
POLICE LOADED TWO BODIES
INTO A PADDY WAGON.

BODY SHOT/PADDY WAGON

BOTH VICTIMS WERE BLACK
MALE TEENAGERS. BOTH
VICTIMS WERE SHOT FIVE
TIMES. TWO AMBULANCES

AMBULANCE/FLASHING LIGHTS

RUSHED TO FELLOWS PARK
WHERE IT HAPPENED SHORTLY
AFTER NINE P.M.
BUT PARAMEDICS SAY WHEN
THEY ARRIVED, THERE WAS
NOTHING THEY COULD DO.
(***STOP/SOT***)

CHYRON NAME:
LEWIS REYNOLDS/PARAMEDIC

"When we got here the victims
were over by the park bench

1

near the baseball diamond.
Blood was everywhere. I knew
they were dead."
(**REPORTER TRACK CONT**)

HIGH SCHOOL YEARBOOK PICTURES:

THE VICTIMS HAVE BEEN
IDENTIFIED AS SIXTEEN-YEAR-
OLD BENJI ADAMS AND
SEVENTEEN-YEAR-OLD LONNIE
HEARD.
BOTH WERE JUNIORS AT JAMES
HOWELL HIGH SCHOOL.

GRAFFITI ON SCHOOL WALL

POLICE SAY BOTH TEENS WERE
MEMBERS OF THE ROCK
DISCIPLES STREET GANG.

CHYRON NAME:
OFC. ALICE WITSOME/CHICAGO PD

(***STOP/SOT***)
"The Rock Disciples and the
Gangster Bandits are feuding
over turf. We don't know what
set off this shooting. They just
kill each other at the drop of a
hat."
(**REPORTER TRACK CONT**)

ROLLING WIDE SHOT OF PARK/PEOPLE
WALKING & KIDS PLAYING

RETALIATION IS LIKELY.
RESIDENTS IN THE
NEIGHBORHOOD SAY MORE
POLICE PATROLS ARE NEEDED
IN THE AREA. UNTIL THEN,
THEY SAY, NO ONE IS SAFE.
GEORGIA BARNETT,
CHANNEL 8 NEWS.

END OF PACKAGE/TIME: 1:30 SECS

*A*nd no one was safe: including me, Georgia Barnett.

That's how it all started. It began when I was sent to cover a story about rival gangs and a double murder in Fellows Park in Englewood. Englewood is a poor and criminally ravaged community on the South Side of Chicago. It was once a strong, working class neighborhood full of people with an immense sense of pride. I should know, it's the neighborhood I grew up in. Some good people live there now but unfortunately crime has gotten outrageous.

That night after my story ran on the 10 P.M. show, I kept looking for angles. I'm a newshound. I love fighting for the lead story. I know that when you get a lead story, you better hold on to it. A lead story is hard to lock down. This is especially true for a black woman reporter. Very often we are underesti-mated, forced to work the fluff stories, pimped. I'm not having it. For me it's a simple case of pride and prejudice—to show some pride, you work around the journalistic prejudice.

Now if you want a hard news story that's a bona fide lead, then, in the words of RuPaul, "Girlfriend, you gotta work!" And I mean work. You run twice as far and twice as fast to win the same prize. I had a hold of a darn good story, but more than that, in this case, I was trying to work my tail off to keep my mind off the fact that I'd just broken up with my boyfriend Max. My man Max.

He is brilliant. Max thought a story and talked a story. He gave you fears and tears. Those are the two things that are guaranteed to keep the remote on Middle America's coffee table. Don't change that channel! Max . . . well . . . the boy is just bad!

Now right this minute I'm going to tell the hon-est-to-Jesus truth. I lost Max to a hoochie mama I couldn't compete with by the name of Emmy—as in the award. She was everything I'm not. A trophy he could handle.

After winning the Emmy award, it was simply TV. TV theme song that is. As in: *Next thing you know old Max is a star. Kinfolks said, Man, move away from there. Said, Network is where you oughta be. So the next thing you know he was movin' to D.C. Global news that is. Overseas. Saddam. Satellites.*

So to forget about my breakup with Max, I focused on the double murder in Fellows Park. Who shot the two Rock Disciples? Members of the rival gang the Bandits, of course. Each day I hustled. I had my news groove on and I was determined to have the best reports on this top story.

I scooped everyone when I found out that the Chicago PD had issued arrest warrants for three members of the Bandits street gang. They were the main suspects, believed to be the shooters. I was on this story like cheese on grits. When two of the Bandits were arrested and charged with murder, I was there and got exclusive pictures. I covered the story all day, fronting it live from the cop shop for the six o'clock and the ten o'clock news. Think that was the end of it? Think again.

ONE

My day seemed to be winding down innocently enough—

"Georgia, may I see you for a minute?"

—but it didn't play out that way.

I stepped into my boss's office. Garbage was everywhere. Crushed tin cans. Stacks of old newspapers. A broken stress toy on the floor. *Stress test flunked, okay.*

I thought of Junk Man, the urban prospector who used to cruise my old neighborhood with a grocery cart. Junk Man loved to sift through garbage. This office would be his treasure island.

"Clear a space somewhere," said my boss, Halo Bingington. "Please have a seat."

Bing's personality is half George Foreman and half Mike Tyson. That's cool for two rock 'em, sock

6

'em boxers but not cool for one newsroom boss. So I knew that Bing's nice-nice stuff could turn ugly quick and in a hurry.

When your boss calls you into his office, you get that *feeling*. Like after the match ignites the fuse in a *Mission Impossible* rerun, I saw scenes flashing before my eyes. They were scenes from my last exclusive.

It was late night and hotter outside than a hole-in-the-wall barbeque joint. The police cars were lined up in front of a frame house. I was on the journalistic down low. Me and my one-man crew crouched in the bushes, waiting for the arrests.

Two Bandits were inside the house. Sammy Sosa could throw a baseball from the front porch and it would probably land near the pitcher's mound in nearby Fellows Park. That's where the bodies had been found, riddled with bullets.

The two suspects were grabbed out of bed, but, true to thug life, they seemed unfazed by the police. Officers yanked them outside by the necks, pajama bottoms sagging, hands cuffed behind their backs with silver bracelets that jingled. It was the only sound in the night. Except cries. One of the suspects' mothers leaned over the porch railing sobbing as she grabbed for her son, a man who had been out of reach for quite some time.

I'd written the story with feelings and facts. I'd fronted it live from the scene. But now something was wrong. The competition couldn't possibly have scooped me on some new development, could they? Did the suspects make bond and I didn't know it?

Did the cops find the murder weapon and I missed it?

I watched my boss, Bing, as he made a quick call. He sat wide-legged, khaki pants high above his bare ankles. Scuffy, comfortable shoes fit loosely on his feet as he bounced his right leg up and down. Small freckled hands drummed on the desk, then Bing stopped and used his left hand to free several strands of dirty blond hair matted against the back of his neck by sweat. Bing finished his call and focused directly on me.

In direct contrast to Bing's warm and rich voice, suddenly his eyes turned cold with displeasure. Bing had started out as a commercial announcer, moved to radio news, then to TV. But he paid the cost to be the boss. Three decades in this business had lost Bing some of his hair, his waistline, his first and second wives, but not his drive to be number one.

"Georgia, your on-camera look stunk. You didn't fix your makeup and your hair was out of place! Channel 14's reporter looked flawless."

I thought of the Generation X babe with Breck hair and poor writing skills. "But, Bing, the competition didn't have the exclusive video of the arrests. They didn't have the kid's mother either. I was hustling like a popcorn vendor at the circus! I was worried about facts, not face."

"Georgia, this is TV news. The viewers care about how you look. You kicked tail on the story but you didn't polish it off. Ratings are about how our reporters look *just as much* as they are about our news coverage."

Bing continued to bawl me out. I listened halfheartedly, then shrugged before heading back out into the newsroom.

"Georgia, Georgia on my mind!" Nancy Haverstein yelled out at me. She's the producer for the ten o'clock news.

"Yeah, Nancy." I smiled. She was actually one of the reasonable ones at my tripped-out television station, WJIV Channel 8 in Chicago. I've been a TV general assignment reporter in four other markets, all in Ohio, before finally getting a break. Then I was able to get-down-boogie-oogie-oogie back home to Chi-town.

My coworkers seem to think that "Georgia, Georgia" is an original joke. The best joke occurred when my twin sister and I were born.

At first my mother named me Georgia and my sister Georgina.

But my grandmother, who in her heyday did musical comedy on the chitlin circuit, went to find the hospital nurse. Grandma told her to change Georgina's name to Peaches. Mama threw a fit. Grandma said then, and still says now, that Mama is always raising saying over nothing.

Mama changed my sister's name back to Georgina but as far as my family was concerned it was far too late. You know how black folks hate to let go of a nickname. Poor Georgina's nickname was stuck to her like paint on a brush. I have to admit, though, I loved going to Savannah and hearing my grandmother call us in from playing: "Georgia, Peaches! Where are my sweet Georgia, Peaches?!"

I walked over to Nancy. She's good people—kind,

even-tempered, considerate, and gently honest. Nancy's fronting on fifty but not looking nearly that age. She has a naturally slender build and bright, taut skin; raven black hair falls three inches below the big hoop earrings she loves to wear. Nancy's eyes are the singed brown color of cigar smoke. She blinks them constantly, too. It's a nervous habit she shoplifted after working in various television newsrooms across the country.

Nancy pointed to the show rundown, which lists the stories included in the newscast. "Take a look, Georgia. I don't have a strong lead. What about a hot-weather story—can you write something cute?"

"Ughh!" I groaned. Don't go there! I would have to stand outside somewhere on Michigan Avenue or along the lakefront and talk about how hot it was—and my hair was surely going to go berserk! Heat and humidity on a black woman's hair? Goodness.

"Georgia, what do you think about doing a weather crawl?"

"A weather crawl? Girl, *do a hair advisory!* Nancy, if you send me outside to do a heat story in this weather, my hair is going to look like I'm a backup singer with Sly and the Family Stone. And you know Bing wears two hats—newsroom boss and chief of the cosmetic police. Dude wants glamour. Bing doesn't care if it's humid or windy or wet. He wants face and hair from his female reporters. But Bing doesn't say a word to the guys! They can look any kind of way. Give me a pass, huh, Nancy?"

Before she could answer, an intern yelled, "Got a breaker! Caller says there's been a drive-by shooting. Five people shot."

"New lead!" Nancy announced to the newsroom. "Hit it, Georgia!"

I hustled to get started on the breaking story. But I got delayed at the front door, waiting for one of our crew trucks to pick me up. I flipped a glance up to the sky, then sighed. The raindrops were steamed by the sun until they became a mist that clung to everyone who stepped out into The Sauna, a Chicago synonym for midday in August.

I put on my thinking brim as I waited for my crew. A drive-by at Fiftieth and Hedge. It was in Englewood, my old neighborhood. A curious feeling came over me—a double-dip emotion of warmth and apprehension. It's hard covering stories in Englewood. The neighborhood has changed so much from the way it was when I was a little kid.

I had already covered the double murder in Fellows Park last week, a park where my twin and I used to play double Dutch and where we sang our first "concert" under the monkey bars, come one come all, for a nickel apiece.

Once again I tried to give myself the proper distance for peace of mind to do my job. Out of the corner of my eye, I caught sight of a Channel 8 truck turning the corner. When I saw who the cameraman was, my heart went *yeah!* and *help me, Lord!* at the same time. It was Zeke Rouster.

Zeke shoots great pictures but he drives like Al Unser on crack. Zeke has long bony legs, a jelly stomach, pale green eyes, and stone white hair. He holds the record among cameramen for the most moving violations. It's not a Channel 8 record, it's the record for the entire city. And Zeke has no shame in his game about it either.

A country boy raised outside of Birmingham, Zeke says his hot-rod days began at twelve years old when he jumped into a beat-up flatbed truck one day and set out driving. His goal was to travel as far as he could, as fast as he could, without knocking down anything that breathed. Zeke is an underachiever; he hasn't killed anything yet and his goal hasn't changed in thirty years.

"Rock and roll!" Zeke said, burning rubber when he hit the brakes and opened the door with one fly-guy motion. As the truck sped toward the crime scene, so did my thoughts and my expectations. Doesn't everyone have some recurring experience that makes them uneasy? Butterflies before making a speech? An anxious anticipation of something? I was nervous as a turkey in November as I fumbled with the metal fringes of my pad.

It's not as if I'm a cub reporter. I've been to violent crime scenes a gazillion times. Sometimes the body is still there. Sometimes there is blood. Sometimes the victim is still alive, grappling with his spirit like a child trying to steer a runaway bike. I'm called upon to make sense out of it for more than 300,000 viewers.

Isn't that a big dog of a responsibility, being the eyes, ears, and conscience of others? How can I ever take it lightly? How can I ever cruise through work? Each day is mentally tough, but I love it. How great is it to be able to tell a story that people want to know about? But the violent news always works my

12

nerves in the beginning. Mentally I got prepared to do my best and deal with the violence by silently saying the Twenty-third Psalm. That got me focused for whatever lay ahead of me on this story. It turned out to be something to pray about and nothing to play with.

TWO

"Over here! Bring the stretcher!"

"Get back! Get back!"

"Damn! I haven't seen this many shell casings since Nam!"

The scene was ugly and chaotic. I know a veteran reporter in Cleveland who says he's been in TV news so long that he doesn't get emotional when he looks at a crime scene. Must be nice. I'd like to borrow his eyeballs right about now.

A block party had just ended when the shooting started. Four metal folding tables were turned over on their sides. A white tablecloth, splattered with blood, was swaddled around a folding chair. I stepped around two cracked plastic plates, a swirl of mushy food staining the ground beneath their edges.

We were the first crew at the scene and that's

always good. But, honey-chile, I knew the competition was smoking a path to get there. My mind spun into high gear. The caller said five people were hit. Were there more? We were a few blocks away from the park where the two gangbangers were killed last week. Was this drive-by retaliation like I thought? How many witnesses were there? Could I get them to talk?

The questions banging around in my mind were interrupted when I saw two people, a man and a young girl, being loaded into an ambulance. Both wore breathing devices that resembled a catcher's mask; the apparatus was hitched behind their ears to protect them from the wild pitch that Death was throwing.

I glanced behind me. Zeke was on the case, panning and zooming with the camera. The strong arm of the law had a choke hold on the scene. There were eight to ten beat cops and three plainclothes detectives plus a couple of evidence techs wearing skintight beige gloves searching the grass for bullet casings.

I looked up to my left and saw groups of people sitting on their front porches watching, first the police, then me. A few of the younger, more eager ones were hanging over their chain-link fences. They didn't seem frightened or angry or unhappy but just really tired. Maybe numb is a better word. A creepy feeling came over me as I realized how difficult it had to be to deal with violence like this on such a regular basis. It had become part of the neighborhood scene like the trees and the corner newsstand.

But the way they did nothing tripped me out.

The violence didn't seem to scare the hell out of these residents enough to make them grab anything they could get their hands on to fight back against the gangbangers. That may seem naive, but to me complacency is naive. Doesn't history prove that action and change go hand in hand? And that's not book knowledge talking, that's street sense, too. You want something to go down, you have to make it happen yourself.

There were a few more pockets of people on the corners, too. In one group, a bunch of little kids were standing around watching the commotion.

In the other group, adults talked amongst themselves. I spotted a tall man in a sweat-stained work shirt, about six-two, wide across the shoulders, standing tensely. I guesstimated his age to be around about forty. His upper-body strength clearly established that he did some heavy lifting for a living. A spit of gray adorned his temples and he was hugging a teenage girl who was crying. I couldn't see her face but I saw his. His eyes looked as if they were throbbing, the anger in them was just that intense. With an arm around the girl's shoulders, he comforted her. I could see the oil stains beneath his nails. His jaw clenched as he gritted his teeth twice.

I was on it. Like radar, my eyes and mind focused in and read the person in front of me. The reporter in me knew that he was my man. It's a tip-off to a reporter: Who is angry? Who is a leader? Who will open up for whatever the reason? That's who a reporter has to find, a needle in a haystack, a good witness in the crowd. That was this dude in front of me. He was pissed off enough to give me the gutsy, for true interview that I needed.

"C'mon!" I told Zeke. We cautiously approached the man I wanted to interview. "I'm sorry to bother you during such a tough time. . . . Can you tell me what happened here?"

The teenager stopped crying for a second, then looked at me for a long moment before her tears began flowing once more. The man gritted his teeth again. "I'll tell you what . . . these gangbangers are shooting up each other and anybody they see. They just missed my cousin Karen here but got her girlfriend Jackie in the chest. Shooting, that's all they know. I'm so tired of it! You can't walk the street, can't have a damn block party for them trying to kill somebody over turf."

"'Them' who?"

"The Bandits and the Rockies."

I'm hip to the nicknames for the Gangster Bandits and the Rock Disciples, two of the most notorious street gangs in Chicago. "Did you get a good look at the car?"

He inhaled deeply, stared a second, then said, "I didn't see *nobody*. . . . I just heard a lot of gunfire."

"What about the direction the car came from?"

The girl wailed and he clutched her tightly, soothing, "It's okay, it'll be okay, sshhhh."

"Sir? Which way did the car come from?"

He waved his free arm wildly. "This way, that way, some kinda way! It just don't make no sense. I'm through."

"I understand how frustrating this is for you. But

if you could answer just a couple more questions—"

"Enough is enough."

Now at this point my reporter instincts kicked in. What kind of body language was this man giving off? How much could I push him? Could I push him? I made a quick assessment of his eyes, his stance, then back to those eyes.

"Okay, thank you." I decided to back off and not blow up the bridge. "Sir, I really appreciate you taking the time to talk to me. For editing purposes, say and spell your full name, please?"

"Calvin Hughes. C-a-l-v-i-n. H-u-g-h-e-s."

I gave Mr. Hughes my card because he could be a good contact to have in the neighborhood. I could hear his cousin continuing to sob. I thought, I feel for you girl. It is so tough to watch people hurt. Even though I see so much of it, I have to stay focused, but that does not mean becoming numb. I don't ever want to go there, because when it gets like that, then it's time to bail. But you've got to do your job. I have to get the story.

I heard my pager go off. I knew it was *them*. The producer was worrying me about going live for the upcoming newsbreak. Zeke and I went back to the truck to set up a signal to air live pictures from the scene.

It works like this: An electronic signal is set up from equipment inside the truck. That signal is locked into a channel of a microwave dish on top of the Sears Tower or the Hancock Center. You can then transmit live pictures or play the tape that you've recorded back over those channels to the station where it's recorded and viewed by a writer and tape editor. Then I write the story and read it back over that same signal, a process called tracking, and the writer and editor put together a long story called a package. Normally I would do all this later, but we were doing a live shot for the newsbreak.

I had about twenty minutes to the newsbreak, so I pulled out my makeup. My sister, Peaches, says I look like an overdone French fry—toasty brown, tall, and lean. I rushed to put on eyeliner because my large chestnut eyes are my pow feature. My hair? Simply put, it was wrecked, getting puffier and puffier by the second. Sorry to say but I was hopeless about the head this day and there wasn't a darn thing I could do about it. I grabbed a clip and pulled my hair back. I didn't look great but I did look presentable. There wasn't a lot of time to fool with myself. Even though this is TV, the story comes first with me.

I put my cosmetics away and began to practice how I would lead into my big story. I was talking it through to myself out loud, "I'm Georgia Barnett, live on the South Side where a neighborhood block party turned into a frightening scene of violence. . . ."

Zeke gave me an internal feedback device or IFB, a little earplug that lets me hear Nancy and the director back at the station. Through the IFB I heard them ask me for a mike check. I counted down for them. My audio was good. I saw that the little children who were on the corner were now crowding around me. They were anywhere between the ages of six and ten.

"We wanna be on! Hip hop hurray-hey, ho-hey!"

one of them shouted and the others joined in waving back and forth at the camera.

"Hold it," I said. "I'm working and I can't put you on television doing that. This is not a music video. So there'll be no 'hip hop hurray-hey, ho-hey!'" I sang it and did the little wave part, too. They got a kick out of that. Even Zeke laughed. "You can stand behind me and be on air but no waving and yelling, okay?"

They agreed, then lined up with starburst smiles in a curbside class picture.

"Coming to you in ten," the director said in my ear through my IFB. I got focused, looking straight into the camera.

"In five, Georgia!" He counted me down. I relaxed my face a little bit. Then the director cued me: "Go!"

"I'm Georgia Barnett, live on the South Side where a neighborhood block party turned into a frightening scene of gang violence. Five people have been shot—"

Suddenly I heard somebody yelling in my ear from the control room back at the station. The director? No. The producer? No.

It was Bing!

He wolfed, "Ask the kids something! Use the fuckin' kids!"

How could I think and talk live in front of thousands of people with Bing yelling in my ear?

"Get a bite from the kids, Georgia!"

I struggled to finish my thought without stuttering live on-air. "There were only a few people outside cleaning up when the drive-by occurred—"

"Use the kids! Now!!!"

I turned to the kids behind me. "Did you see anything?"

A cute little girl with fuzzy-plaited hair was standing in front. She was wearing a faded pink and white sleeveless cotton dress. Large eyes brimming with excitement focused on me. The little girl grabbed the mike and said, "I seent a car. This real dark black boy with a scar, he was dressed all in yellow, and just shooting his gun!"

An ashy hand belonging to a little boy with a jealous heart grabbed the mike away from her. He shouted, "Let me talk some! They were shooting, I was running! Bang! Bang!"

Now the rest of the kids went off the deep end, too: "Bang! Bang!"

Bing was in my ear again, yelling, "Wrap! Wrap!"

"Again, there's been a drive-by shooting on the South Side. Five people shot. We'll have a report from the scene and from the hospital. Channel 8 News will have all the latest details at ten."

I stood very still until I knew I was no longer live on the air, then I threw down my mike and cursed, "Dap-gum-it!"

All the kids scattered, mocking me: "Dap-gum-it!"

"Zeke, Bing was yelling in my ear the entire live shot. I could barely think. He totally messed me up. Now all the viewers think I don't know what I'm doing. But how can I do my job with a domineering boss yelling in my ear?"

Zeke just shrugged.

Then the phone rang in the truck. I didn't need to dial 1-800-Psychic to know that it was Bing. I wasn't about to take any more mess off Mr. News-it-all. I moved toward the phone inside the truck.

Zeke stopped me. "Don't bother, Georgia. Bing will only piss you off. Let's hustle up."

Zeke was right. I needed to finish up what I had to do, and quickly, because the other stations had started to arrive at the scene. Zeke popped in a new tape and we got ready to flag down one of the cops handling this shooting. I was trying my darndest to swallow my anger and get focused when I caught sight of a newcomer to the scene, a calming force in the chaos.

I slowly approached this stunning man. He was an ab- and back-plus masterpiece, his mountainous shoulders tapering down to a just-right waist. Obviously he believed in caring for his body. An overall rugged look was softened perfectly by his creamy reddish-brown skin. Mister-man squared his shoulders, spoke firmly, and gave orders as naturally as exhaling. His figure and his confidence cut a magnificent presence among the madness.

Who was he? I hadn't seen him on any of the other murder stories I'd covered. Clearly he was *somebody*, or he would be soon. Could he help me with this story? I went straight over and introduced myself. "Georgia Barnett, 8 News. I'd like to talk to you about the investigation."

He barely glanced in my direction. Mister-man was cool as the underside of a pillow. He said in a voice aged in a wine cellar, "I'm Detective Doug

Eckart. And I'm busy." Then he ignored me good old fashion. Detective Eckart turned and began talking to a beat cop who was now standing next to him.

"Excuse me, Detective," I said louder, more forcefully. "I'd like to do a quick interview with you."

"Nope."

He didn't even look at me. "Too busy. I can't be bothered right now."

Well, in the words of Chaka Khan, Please pardon me! Sometimes these detectives are super-helpful because they know we can assist them by asking the public for information. But sometimes old-school detectives don't like to cooperate with us. They think we're too glitzy or that we're nothing but a pain in the behind. But this guy wasn't old enough to have that kind of Jurassic 'tude! What was his problem? He had a job to do and so did I—and I only wanted to help and that's all my news report would do.

"Detective Eckart," I said firmly but politely, "I'm not asking for an extensive sit-down. I just want you to spot me up on what's happening in a quick one-on-one. In return, any info I may get I'll pass along to you. You know how it works."

"In a few minutes I'll do an interview with everybody. I'll just get it over with then. Okay?"

Not okay! An interview with everyone? With all the other TV stations, radio, and newspaper reporters, too? Excuse the pun, but a gangbang was what we called it in the business. What made him think I'd settle for something as common as all that? I don't think so, Detective Eckart. I wanted an exclusive interview, a shot of us walking together to show

23

that I was here first, that I had the best stuff—I wanted to strut that stuff.

"Excuse me, Detective Eckart?"

He looked at me, annoyed. "Detective, I hustled to get here and I've got a lot of great stuff. I just want to cap it all off with a quick interview with you. Five minutes. My cameraman is right here, you can walk the block with me and tell me about this turf war. Otherwise, we'll just hang around on your heels."

"That's all you reporters tend to do—hang around on our heels getting in the way." Detective Eckart snorted.

"It seems to me that because we're in the way, most of your cases get solved because we make people aware of what's going on. We're really not in the way, we're helping *make* a way."

To outsiders it would appear that we were now engaged in a stare-down. But it wasn't. It was a momentary mesh of understandings, the art of give and get. He realized that he must give to get me out of his way.

Detective Eckart suppressed a cough in the low end of his throat, then showed me his bad-cop scowl. "Five minutes and that's it, understood?"

"Understood."

We let Zeke swing around in front. That way he would have a walking shot of us together. I started by asking a question I knew the answer to. I wanted to get a read on this man's body language. That way I would be able to pick up on habits that would distinguish truths from lies.

"Detective Eckart, could this drive-by be retaliation for the two murders that happened in the park last week?"

"That's exactly what we think it is. It's a tit-for-tat deal that the gangs love to play with one another."

Truthful: straight gaze, no eye or eyebrow movement, no change in walking stride.

"Do you have any suspects?"

"No, we don't have any suspects and no one in custody to be questioned."

Truthful: straight gaze, no eye or eyebrow movement, no change in walking stride.

"What about leads? Any clues to point you guys in a specific direction?"

"No, we do not have any leads at this time. But our investigation is moving forward."

Lying: eyes dart quickly, slight hitch in the walk before resuming stride.

"If we get any big developments in the case, we'll hold a news conference to brief reporters. Right now I have no hard details."

Lying: eyes dart quickly, slight hitch in the walk before resuming stride.

Obviously that was about all I was gonna get out of him and that wasn't much. So I decided to get an extra sound bite on the history of the gangs for my story.

"How quickly is the gang problem growing in Chicago?"

"There are 125 gangs with more than 100,000 members. It's not a mom-and-pop thing either. They're all organized. Each gang has hand signs, colors, and graffiti symbols."

"How did the Gangster Bandits and the Rockies get started?"

"Well, the Gangster Bandits are just an old gang with a new name. We break 'em down, they regroup, and come back under a new name."

"And the Rockies?"

"The Rockies are different," Detective Eckart explained. "They started in the South which is unusual; it's often the other way around. But a couple of Rockies living in Arkansas came to Chicago about ten years ago and started up a branch here. Now each side has their turf—Bandits have the streets east of Fellows Park on Vincennes. The Rockies have the streets west of the park."

"The park itself is divided up the same way, right?"

"Yes, east side is Bandits and west side is Rockies. But now they're spilling over from block to block, which is extremely chaotic. The area leaders—they call them governors or lieutenants—are responsible for territory. Both sides have weak leadership. That's the problem. That's what triggered the double homicide in Fellows Park. A stupid turf war."

"There are two suspects charged in that murder, correct?"

"Right," Detective Eckart answered. "Both suspects are being held on half a million dollars bond. A third suspect remains at large."

"Are gang-related homicides on the rise?"

"Yes. Last year there were 930 murders in Chicago and 34 percent of those homicides were gang related."

Detective Doug Eckart stopped walking and looked at his watch. "Five minutes are up."

"You're fast."

A playful smirk crossed his face. "No, you're slow."

I couldn't resist a purr. "Ah . . . not really, Detective."

He looked at me and a smile crept into his eyes. "Maybe not."

Zeke had stopped shooting and was changing tapes. "Just another minute, Detective. I need a couple of cutaway shots, okay guys?"

We both nodded as Zeke began walking around, getting video of us standing together. We looked at each other so Zeke could get a reverse angle shot and Detective Eckart's eyes gave off a silky threaded gaze. Our silence was flirtatious. Then for a more animated shot, but really to break that awkward silence, I asked a question.

"This gang war is about to blow up, don't you think?"

Detective Eckart's bushy eyebrows humped together like a big M as he glanced down at my hand. I killed the mike I held. Then he answered.

"Hell, yeah. If we don't calm this thing down these young men will start killing each other like crazy. I hate to see these young brothers dying for nothing. It gets tougher and tougher to make a difference, but we're not going to give up trying."

In those last few words, I saw a change in Detective Eckart. His voice softened as he spoke and there was more emotion coming from him. "This

case in particular gives me a nasty feeling in my gut."
A sadness flashed briefly in his eyes.

"What's that, Detective?"

"The rest of this summer is going to go out with
a lot of bloodshed."

"Let's hope not."

"Yeah." He sighed, pulling out a handkerchief to
dab at the sweat trickling down his ear before showing me his good-cop smile and walking away. "See ya
around."

After he left, Detective Eckart's aura lingered.
He was an impressive man, smart, seemingly not too
jaded by his job, and I hoped that he would be able to
help me with this case. Plus he had a presence about
him that made me want to get to know him better.

After the interview I wrote my story. Later, I was
live at the top of the ten o'clock news. After that,
Zeke and I began to wrap up. Hanging around in the
old neighborhood, seeing again how it has changed
for the worse, stirred up some feelings I needed to
share. And there was only one person I wanted to
share those feelings with.

THREE

___

Sweet-sweet-sweet home, Chah-caaah-go!"

I was pretty close to my sister's place over on Pershing Road, so when we packed up our gear after the ten o'clock show I asked Zeke to drop me off over there. I wanted to talk to my twin—we could talk and argue about anything in the universe. I could hear Peaches singing as I approached the entrance of her joint, the Blues Box.

"Sweet-sweet-sweet home, Chah-caaah-go!"

My twin can *swang* the blues. Peaches has a torch for a throat. Imagine Gladys Knight's gritty kind of a voice with Patti LaBelle's power. Peaches and I are fraternal twins, not identical. From the git-go we looked alike until about, oh, age six, when I went up and Peaches went out. Some people say she's fat but I say she's sexy-solid with big hips, legs, and boobs. Peaches has a big attitude, too. We are certainly twins in that respect.

When Peaches wanted to buy the place on Pershing Road she showed it to Mama and me first. One: she wanted our two cents. Two: she wanted our ten grand.

I remember that overcast day very well, even though it was three years ago. The Chicago wind had its teeth out biting and tearing through our coats as Mama, Peaches, and I stood in front of the shuttered tavern that would one day be the Blues Box.

The neighborhood reminded me of a dapper old lady who can't quite keep up appearances anymore. You know, rusty yet showing signs of the regalness that once was. The block was lined with beautifully constructed buildings, but all were boarded up. I mean six of the ten businesses on the block were closed; the other four included a Laundromat, a liquor store, a cleaners, and a grocery store. But it was an easy-to-get-to kind of a place off Lake Shore Drive and it was reasonably close to Hyde Park, the upscale integrated community on the South Side where the University of Chicago is located.

"It's got a lot of potential," Peaches reasoned.

"Which means it ain't nothing now," Mama observed.

Mama can be battle-ax blunt when she wants. Mama feels she's earned the right to be, especially when it comes to show business because of all the drama she went through trying to make it big in her younger days. She failed miserably.

"Sweeet-sweeet home, Chah-caaah-go!"

I looked up at my sister through the glass window as I reached the doorway. Dog, it's amazing what Windex, a rag, paint, and a brush can do. Peaches spent pennies on rehabbing the building and the old girl cleaned up nicely. That turned out to be a good thing, too, because the rest of the money she borrowed went toward setting up the bar, kitchen, and eventually to keeping the place open. Business, sad to say, was not booming.

I stepped inside the Blues Box and, as usual, the first person I laid eyes on was Milton, an old played-out musician who collects the cover charge. Milton had his Dobbs hat broke down over his left eye. He was sitting on a lopsided stool with his long legs stretched across the side of the doorway. With a chewed-up cigar dangling from his lips, Milton was so busy gawking at Peaches that he didn't even see me standing there.

Milton is a down-home harmonica man with sixty years in the blues business, beginning when he first stepped onto a Memphis stage at age ten. They say in his day he could make a woman faint just by playing a love song on his harmonica. Milton still calls the harmonica his best leg.

"Sang-sang," he hummed out, popping his fingers. Peaches had to bawl out Milton to stop him from letting in free every woman he thought was pretty. Pretty to an old dude like Milton is practically any woman under seventy who walked without a cane. Finally he looked up at me. Milton winked and gave me his trademark greeting: "Go'ne in and let the good times roll!"

The place was fairly crowded for a weeknight and I know that was part of the reason Peaches was singing so well. The more money she made the better she sounded. Good! Maybe she could start paying me back some of the mercy money I had loaned her to start up this joint. Mercy money is what I call the cash in my emergency account; it's there to ease the pain of a personal or family crisis.

I walked inside the club and was met next by lanky, elegant Rita, the club hostess. She's a real south-side belle, twirling gold wrist bangles and sipping Tanqueray with a twist. She made a big to-do out of seating me at the reserved house table next to the stage. Peaches saw me and started to show off. I hate to admit it but I like it when she shows off for me at the club.

My twin's voice got more volume to it, her shake got sexier, and her band started really booming. When she finished up, Peaches's rinse cycle was set on sweat. She grabbed a glass of cranberry juice and lifted it to acknowledge the applause as she came over and sat down at my table.

"Hey, Peaches!"

"Sister-twin!" she said, and we kissed and hugged. "'Bout time you brought your skinny butt in here to see me."

"I'm sorry, Peaches, but I've been so busy."

"So what, you still could have called!"

"Why didn't you call me then?"

Peaches laughed and winked sarcastically. "I've got to save my voice, don'tcha know. I'm the talented one and you the smart one, remember?"

Obviously she and Mama had gotten into it today at some point and put me in the middle of it. Mama had a bad habit of throwing up my success in Peaches's face. But I didn't come here for conflict. I'd had a hard day, so I let that little snap pass. "Just shut up and buy me a drink on the house."

"Holy moly, Georgia!" Peaches laughed and began teasing. "You know I love you but—no freebies here. You're gonna have to work for that drink. Let's have some fun!"

"Girl, I don't feel like playing around!"

"Sister-twin, I know you don't court the stage—found that out when you broke up the act! But c'mon! Shake a tail feather!"

Then Peaches bolted from the table. Oh God! I tried to snatch her out of that skintight dress but I missed. Peaches grabbed one of the mikes and announced, "Ladies and gents, we've got a special something for you tonight."

I waved frantically, *no!*

Peaches saw me and sucked her teeth, in the mike no less, before saying, "My sister is here tonight. Many of you know her from Channel 8; she's the hottest . . . smartest . . . best-looking television reporter in town. . . . Georgia Barnett!" Peaches then did a bump, a grind, and a double point over at me.

I waved, feeling good that Peaches wanted to do

some boisterous bragging on me. But every time she did, she'd come right behind all that good and embarrass me. I knew it was coming, that's why I tried to stop her. But stopping Peaches was like trying to stop a runaway train with your big toe.

"We're twins. Fraternal. Georgia is the oldest!"

"By a minute!" I shouted.

The crowd laughed.

"I want her to come up here and play the piano for you!"

The crowd was cheering me on and I was so embarrassed, but what could I do? I walked over to the piano, sat down, and played—"Mary Had a Little Lamb."

Everyone laughed at me and I started laughing myself. Then Peaches started to scat . . . up two octaves above the key I was playing in. She was working it! Peaches is bad! I dropped in a few notes of harmony myself because I've got a good, can-do choir voice but nothing that can compare to my sister's serious solo voice with its range, depth, and feeling. I took the high end of the temporary duet when the band joined in—then I faded out to let my sister roll. Peaches was born to sing, and I love hearing her blow any chance I get.

We were both soggy with sweat when we finally took our seats again. "Georgia," Peaches slurred from fatigue, "we cut up but some good that time! Huh? Whatcha say, whatcha say?"

We did sound good but we both knew that our performing days together were long gone. Every now and then, though, we liked to sing a few songs together.

"Hey, Peaches," I said toweling my forehead off with a rough-edged napkin. "I was back in the old neighborhood today."

"Yeah? Who done shot who now?"

"*You know?* That's how I felt when the story broke. Englewood wasn't like that when we were kids. The neighborhood just blew up! It is a mess over there now. The candy store is gone. There's a vacant lot where the barbershop used to be. I feel displaced and out of touch every time I visit now."

"Georgia," Peaches said, waving her hand for the bartender, who promptly brought over a glass of honey and a spoon. "It's crazy. People started moving out. Jobs got scarce. Crime started rising. But face it; life is about change whether we can get with it or not. Don't spaz about it though. Just do your thing, report the news."

"Yeah, Peaches, you're right. Say, I know you keep your ear to the ground. Any of our old school buddies still hanging out in the old hood?"

"Why?" Peaches grunted as she swallowed down a big spoon of honey. "I'm not trying to get anybody in trouble."

"Am I the law? I just want to have an ear inside the community. Maybe somebody can give me an extra tip or two on this gang thing happening over there."

"Well, there are still a couple of people, just not on the old block. Ms. Liza—she's in that old-folks' home the city just built on Parnell Street. A.J.'s mama is still there but she's sick, mostly house-bound."

"Hmmmmm. What about A.J.?"

"Get that 'suckey' out your voice, sister-twin. A.J. is a crack fiend now."

"*What?* I hate that. A.J. was smart. And he was always protecting everybody, looking out for the little ones and the weak ones. And he was so fine, too. Like a knight in shining black armor!"

Peaches snorted. "Humphf! You know you wanted to give that boy some panties when you were seventeen but you were just too scared."

"Forget you." I cut my eyes at Peaches.

"Remember I was dating his friend, super-fine Sidney, but I wasn't the scary type, don'tcha know!"

We both laughed, then high-fived each other.

"Peaches you were such a fast girl! We just knew you were going to turn up pregnant!"

"Nah!" Peaches laughed, "I fooled y'all. I waited till I was an old lady in my thirties before I had my baby Satch. But damn if I don't wish I was still hanging with Sidney. I heard boyfriend is an accountant in Atlanta now, happily married, and doing real well."

"That's nice, wish A.J. could have turned out like that. Does he still live with his mother?"

"Naw, she put A.J. out because he was acting crazy. A.J.'s living on the street he says. I know 'cause he stops by here every now and then. I buy him some food in exchange for him sweeping up. Never mentioned it before because it's so sad to see someone you grew up with hit bottom."

36

After that I tried to relax. I enjoyed the rest of my night at the club clowning with Peaches and accepting free drinks from the regulars. My thoughts, of course, slipped away to my story—the retaliation drive-by for the double murder in Fellows Park. I wondered to myself, What's going to jump off next, and when?

FOUR

The "when" turned up two days later.

It had been two days since the drive-by shooting and I hadn't had a lead story since.

I had called the cop shop every couple of hours. Nothing new, they said. No ID on the suspects, which meant there was no lead story there.

I had called the hospital. Of the five shooting victims, three were still being cared for. One, a teenage girl, remained listed in critical condition. No lead story there, either. Nothing but update material for an anchor to voice-over file tape of the original shooting.

I had even called Detective Eckart hoping to coax something out of him. It would be a long shot, but I can't count how many times nagging a long shot has ended up helping me turn a tough story.

I pictured Detective Eckart each time I called—
handsome, gruff, but caring. I couldn't help but find
him interesting, especially after those flirtatious
looks. But don't you know he didn't return any of my
calls? I stared at the phone on my desk. Should I try
him again? After a few minutes of indecision, I
decided to call him just one more time. I reached for
the phone just as it started ringing.

"Uggggh-huh-huh . . ." was all I heard when I
picked up. Two things I could distinguish immediately—one, it was a woman's voice, and two, she'd
lost it.

"Hello?" I asked. "Who is this? What's wrong?" I
got focused because whoever was on the line was
very afraid and very on edge. "Take a deep breath
and pick your words carefully. Speak slowly."

"My baby . . . is . . . miss . . . ing . . . she gone."
Emotion forced the woman's words out in a mis-
shapen sentence.

Oh God, some poor woman whose child was
missing. I thought of my three-year-old nephew,
Satch, Peaches's boy, and thought of how upset we
would all be if he were missing.

"Ma'am? Ma'am!" I said, trying to calm her.
"Take deep breaths. Now wait and just listen. Let's
start over. First, what's your name?"

"Kelly Stewart. My baby missing and she don't
be going off by herself no time and won't nobody—"

"Kelly, Kelly! Stop a sec. I need you to try to
calm down. I know it's tough. Here, try this: Just
answer my questions and that way I'll be able to get
all the facts, okay?"

"Oh-oh-oh- . . . kay."

I grabbed a pen. "Now, Kelly, where do you live?"

"Fifty-fifteen South Hedge."

She lived in the neighborhood where the drive-by happened two days ago.

"What's your daughter's name?"

"We named her Kelly, afterah me, her last name is Johnson, afterah her daddy, but ev'rbahdy call her Butter 'cause she love bread and butter sammiches."

"How long has Butter been missing?"

"Since yes'day evening and I called the police but they ain't wanna come out here and do nothing. Won't nobody help me and then the kids say you was out here the other day and was real nice so I thought . . ."

"How old is Butter?"

"She six."

"Are you married, divorced, or a single mother?"

"Single mother."

"Could Butter be with her father? Maybe he stopped by and got her and didn't ask—"

"No, he's in the army, stationed overseas."

"Could Butter be at a friend's house, with another relative, something like that?"

"All her friends live in the neighborhood and they ain't seen her, and all our relatives in the city live right here, in this house—my mama, my sister, her son, me, and Butter. We done searched everywhere. She ain't been to see her daddy's people in the South but twice and Butter don't know nothing about getting down there."

"Okay, who did you talk to at the police station?"

"Sergeant . . . uh-uh . . . Reynolds, then I talked to a Sergeant McGuire . . ."

I knew McGuire. He was a bit moody but always straightforward. I had talked to him a couple of times today when I called about the drive-by.

". . . and nobody wanted to help me! Butter is a good girl, too. Butter gets awards in school and in church. Spelling champion. Perfect attendance. Damn, don't y'all get it? My baby is a good girl and she's missing!"

This kid, Butter, didn't sound like a runaway. "Okay, Kelly? Kelly, hang on. I'm with you. Let me go talk to my managers here at the station about coming out to do a story—"

"Thank-you-thank-you-thank-you!"

"I'm not making any promises, Kelly, but I'll do what I can and I hope everything will turn out okay. Give me your number and I'll call you back." I wrote down the number and hung up the phone.

I walked over to the assignment desk where the managing editor and the assignment editor usually sit. It's the hub of the newsroom and it's set off with maps, police and fire scanners, computers, and things needed to make quick decisions on what to cover, who to send, and how to get there. My managing editor and assignment editor are both white men. They were sitting there with Bing, also a white man, discussing a special project for next month. The top decision-makers at WJIV are all white men.

"Hey, guys, I just talked to a woman named Kelly Stewart. Her daughter is missing." I relayed the facts I had, which included where the family lived. "I want to do a story."

Bing, the senior manager, scoffed, "Well, I say no, kids like that are always getting into trouble and running away."

"Kids like what, Bing?"

"You know, kids that *live there*. We can't do a story every time some kid in the ghetto runs away from a bad home."

I wanted to go upside Bing's head. How cheap. How insulting. Instead, I inhaled and exhaled sweetly. "So, you're assuming because this is a poor black child that she's in trouble or she's a runaway? That's . . ."

I paused. I started to say "racist" but that word would set Bing off on a defensive pattern that I didn't want to deal with right now. And it was clear that the other two managers sitting there were not going to help me. As usual, there was a big gap in understanding between me and the white boys, a gap as wide as a crater left behind by an earthquake.

". . . that's a common assumption and surely you all are above that in this wonderful, fair, and impartial newsroom in which we work."

I could tell from their looks that I hadn't drawn blood. I had to make a decision: throw a fit or try another angle. "The point is, guys, that the family lives in the same area where the drive-by was two days ago. If I go cover this story, that gets me points with the people in the neighborhood, which builds contacts and sources for future stories. I'll need that help because Detective Eckart told me off camera that he thinks a major turf war is about to erupt."

I got them where they live.

"Well," Bing said, "maybe we'll run the kid's picture with a description. Maybe a sound bite, *if* it's good. Just do a quick hit on the story and not a long package. Yeah, check it out."

Believe, receive, and run!

I got out of that newsroom as fast as I could. I stopped only to call Kelly. I told her three things:

One: I was on my way.

Two: I needed photos of Butter and I wanted to interview as many members of the family as I could.

Three: I would do my best to keep her story on the air, in the public eye. Heat like that would help solve Butter's disappearance faster.

I was overjoyed. The roller-coaster ride of news was on the upswing. What I didn't know was that it was headed down—quick and in a hurry—as soon as I got the next phone call.

FIVE

The phone began ringing in the truck; Zeke and I were in the express lane headed south on the Dan Ryan. Zeke was trying to beat the sleek el train that runs between the multilanes of traffic stretching north and south. We were smokin' the race when I answered the phone.

"Hi." It was Nancy. "There's a change in plans. We've gotta package this new missing kid story for the six o'clock, plus a live shot and package for the ten o'clock."

"That's great, Nancy. That's what I wanted to do all along. I really have a gut feeling about this little girl Butter—"

"Not her. There's another missing kid. In Hyde Park. You're closest. The other missing kid story is dead."

"Oh, c'mon!" I shouted. "You're not going to pull this!"

"Don't jump on me," Nancy said in a slow and deliberate voice. "Bing and the guys asked me to call and tell you because obviously they knew you'd be upset. But listen, this kid missing in Hyde Park is apparently the eight-year-old son of a University of Chicago professor, a Nobel Prize–winning chemist. It's a big deal. The police are already at the family's house."

"So how long has the boy been missing?"

"Five hours."

"Five hours," I said, gritting my teeth. Then I asked a question that I knew the answer to: "Is he white?"

Nancy didn't say a mumbling word.

"So, this little white boy comes up missing for just five hours and we automatically deem it a story, and a lead story no less. But when this little black girl is missing we don't want to do the story because black kids *allegedly* come up missing all the time. I guess little Butter has the wrong skin color, lineage, and zip code. Three strikes and little Butter is out, huh?"

"Don't beat me up, Georgia. All of the other stations are hot on this U of C missing kid story. It's the lead. And you gotta hustle because we can't get beat, either."

An idea flashed through my head. "Nancy, why not do both stories? A double lead."

"I'm tight on time. I just don't have room in my show for both. Besides, Bing said he told you the story was weak but go ahead and check it out just to build up your contacts in the neighborhood. With the little information you have, it just doesn't hold up as a double lead."

"Of course not. A double lead would be too much like right. God, Nancy . . . this woman is going nuts about her little girl. I already called her and said that I was coming. What am I going to tell her, huh? What can I possibly say to that girl's mother?"

"I know," Nancy said soothingly. "I know."

I was sunk. I had no out. I got the address and more info on this new story from Nancy. I moved the phone away from my ear and told Zeke, "Head to Hyde Park." Then I dialed Butter's mother. I had the foul task of telling her I wasn't coming.

"Why?" Kelly moaned over the phone, emotion bubbling to the surface. "I got the pictures. And we're all here ready to talk. Please come!"

What could I say to her? How could I explain the mechanics and prejudices of how news is covered? In a thirty-minute newscast, there's only about sixteen minutes of real news. Weather and sports get three minutes apiece, the commercial breaks add up to five minutes, chat and cutesy stories eat up the rest. Then the stories picked are either tragic, or scandalous, or affect a wide group of people like big layoffs, blizzards, school strikes, or tampering cases, stuff like that. Missing people were always low on the list but sometimes families with money or fame or contacts can get instant airplay. It's difficult to admit that today this kind of crap is still going on.

I promised Kelly that I would try to help in some

way. She called me a "low-down bitch" and hung up. I didn't say a word for the rest of the drive to Hyde Park. Zeke just glanced over at me periodically. Luckily the good Lord had blessed him with enough common sense to know that I was pissed off and not to mess with me about it.

We pulled up to the house and the news trucks of the other stations were already there. Obviously I was being sent late to the story. I was behind. I hate getting beat on a story!

Zeke and I headed up the walkway of this grand mansion, landscaped with expensive shrubs and rock designs. As we got halfway to the door it flew open and the professor came running out, followed by a woman I assumed was his wife. They were tailed by reporters and camera crews from the other stations. "Roll! Roll!" I shouted to Zeke as I instantly reversed direction.

Zeke backpedaled the way we'd just come, shooting the scene all the while.

We had great position: the professor had to pass right by me. When he got close, I stuck my mike in his face. "Professor, what's going on?"

The man was giddy. "They found my little boy. He rode off on his bike. They have him at the police station at Fifty-first and Wentworth!"

"Your son's safe and unharmed?"

"Yes! Thank God, yes!"

The professor jumped into his car and we shot more video of him driving off. Now all the crews scrambled to their trucks and headed for the police station to get the reunion picture—the capper to the story, the moment he sees his little boy and hugs him. Everyone would be live from the cop shop. I called back to the station and told them what happened and where we were headed. I felt so much better. Now the Hyde Park kid was found. We'd get the reunion picture, I'd write a short package, go live with it from the cop shop at six. Then I could fight for doing Butter's story for the ten o'clock news, which is our bigger audience anyway.

Hey-now, I felt like my luck was changing.

Everything went as planned. We got the huggy-kissy picture we wanted of the little boy and his dad. We got a shot of the red bike with the high-mounted handlebars; the little boy grinning, two teeth missing in the front, holding his Batman action figure.

As soon as we wrapped, I saw Detective Doug Eckart. The man actually looked better than he did when I first met him. He was leaning against a corner wall near the front desk reading a report on the counter. One hand was up cupping his head and the other arm was resting on the counter. His sleeves were up, the flat folds of white resting against the tan muscles of his arms. I walked over to him. I needed help.

I stuck out my hand. "Remember me?"

"Yes." He smiled warmly. "I remember my five-minute exclusive."

"But you don't remember to return phone calls?"

He dropped his head and chuckled. "I'm sorry. I've been swamped."

"Okay, well why not make it up to me then—"

"Sorry, I'm not working the professor's case so I can't give you an interview."

"No, I'm all set on that. Anything new with the drive-by?"

"No suspects in custody," he said, and I watched his body posture get a little stiff and guarded. I was talking about his case now. He got super-serious in a heartbeat.

"But you know who you're looking for?"

"I don't have anything for you right now." His voice was serious but his eyes were smiling.

"C'mon, Detective. Did the evidence at the scene turn up anything? Anything at all?"

"I've got some paperwork to do."

"Wait," I said, stepping in his path. He drew back, seemingly amused, and I felt as if he was toying with me, but not maliciously.

"I need a favor."

"I told you," Detective Eckart said, moving around me, gently touching my shoulder.

"No, this has nothing to do with the drive-by. There's another child missing. A little girl named Butter. She's been missing for about twenty-four hours. Her mother, Kelly, called police and they wouldn't do anything. Then she called me. She was hysterical. I had promised to cover the story and they blew me out of it to do this one. Butter lives over at Fiftieth and South Hedge."

"That's the hot zone. Bandits' and Rockies' territory."

"I know. My bosses didn't want to cover her story because they assumed that a poor little black girl in that kind of neighborhood is a runaway or a troublemaker and it's wasted air time."

Detective Eckart grunted sympathetically.

"Of course I fought to cover her disappearance, but early on I lost. Now with this case wrapped up, I'm planning to go over to Butter's house and finally do her story."

"You're a scrapper," he said admiringly.

"You bet. If I don't fight for this story it won't get done. I'm determined."

"Good."

"But I need help from you, Detective. I was wondering if you could ask the squads in the area to look around for her? Maybe get a beat cop to talk to the mother? If you ask, they'll do it. It's just that we, the media, and you guys, the police, pulled out all the stops for this little boy and no one wants to give the time of day to Butter."

"Except you," Detective Eckart said, his voice relaxing as he leaned against the wall again. "And now me. Sure I'll alert a couple of the guys. Give me the name and address of the family."

"Thank you, Detective," I said, writing down the information for him.

"Doug is fine."

"And you can call me Georgia. I owe you one."

"I collect all my debts, too."

His voice sounded so cute I raised an eyebrow. "Oh you do?"

"Yes, ma'am," he said folding up the paper I'd written the information down on. Doug winked, "See ya."

I wanted to stop him, make him stay, talk to him a bit longer. "Any witnesses in the drive-by?"

Doug stopped and gave me an incredibly straight face.

"C'mon, Doug, there's no camera here. Give me something. A little something so I can stay on top of this story."

Doug smiled slyly and said, "Can I trust you?"

"Ask around."

"Oh, I did," he offered solemnly.

"What? I know my rep is solid." Then his gorgeous eyes softened. He was playing with me again.

"Let's just say that we have an idea of who we want to talk to."

"You wouldn't want to go on camera and tell me that, wouldya?"

Doug stonewalled, crossing his arms in front of him. "You're pushing your luck again, lady."

"Okay, okay . . . thanks again for helping Butter. I'm going to call her mother with the good news now."

"Fine, you just do that," Doug said wistfully.

I ran back to the news truck and called Butter's mother, Kelly. It took a few minutes for her to warm up to me but she was very happy when I told her the police would be by soon to help. While I had her on the phone I got a description of Butter for the story I was planning to railroad through for the ten o'clock news. I had made up my mind to fight for it despite how bad the humbug might become. I was thinking knockout. Muhammad Ali mode. Float like a butterfly and all that jazz.

I was repeating Butter's description as I wrote it down. "Four feet tall, thin, brown eyes and brown hair. Hair in little braids. Wearing a pink and white dress, torn."

Kelly said, "You remember her, don't you? She's the little girl you interviewed!"

I recalled the events of that day and struggled to picture the little girl. *Oh wait!* Then I got an ugly connection in my mind. "Kelly, let me get back to you, okay?"

I hung up the phone and yelled, "Zeke!"

"What?" he yelled back. Zeke came from around the other side of the truck. He was holding a long black strand of cable used to set up our live shot. Zeke's right arm went up like a waiter holding a tray and he began looping the cable around his open palm and his elbow so it could be stored easily.

"Did you record that newsbreak I did at the drive-by?"

"No, I didn't have time. But I had them roll on it back at the station. I always like to grab the tape later to take a peek, to make sure I got you guys lookin' good."

"Is it here in the truck?"

"Yeah, it's here, somewhere." Zeke started searching through a stack of black Beta tapes on the floor of the live truck. "Here!" he said, holding it up. Then he played it for me.

"Cue it up again!" I ran back inside the cop shop and grabbed Doug by the arm. "You've got to see something."

The urgency in my voice forced him to follow. We reached the news truck and I told Zeke, "Play it."

There I was and there was little Butter on tape.

"I seent a car. This real dark black boy with a scar, he was dressed all in yellow, and just shooting his gun!"

Zeke looked at us and we looked at Zeke. He rewound the tape, played it again, then froze it.

"That's the missing girl, Doug. That's Butter."

Doug's face lost a shade of color and gained a stony cast. "Butter saw the shooter and admitted being a witness on live television. That's how the word got out on the street who the shooter was in the drive-by. Now the one person who really saw it all and could be a witness in court is missing."

"Tell me again, Doug, which gang uses the color yellow?"

"The Rockies. That's our suspect, a top-ranking punk in the Rockies. I'm going to Butter's house to see her mother."

"That makes two of us," I said. "Because I'm right on your heels."

SIX

*B*utter Where Are U?

That was the message written in white chalk on the sidewalk in front of the two-story frame house where Butter lived.

Butter Where Are U?

All the other front porches on the block were crowded with people because it was too hot to be cooped up inside. But no crowd was on the front porch of Butter's house. There was no one.

Doug and I stopped at the gate and waited for Zeke to get all of the equipment out of the truck. Doug used a hankie to wipe the sweat off his neck. "Damn, it's hot!"

It was, too. The air seemed to bubble inside my lungs every time I took a breath. But I wasn't thinking about the heat. I was thinking about Butter. Dog,

I was feeling guilty as the devil. I was the one who put Butter on-air. Yes, Bing was yelling in my ear and he said to go with it but I'm no rookie reporter. I didn't start doing this at sunrise today. I'm a veteran and I should have just pulled my earplug out and done the live shot the way I wanted to; the way I planned to. But Bing is my boss and he'll have major input on whether or not I sign a new contract with WJIV. It makes me angry that I have to cater to him and his bogus news ideas but what can I do? It's his newsroom. I can only buck him so much and survive.

Butter Where Are U?, I read again.

Was she alive? Did they kill her? I'd been thinking about that on the way over. Finally, standing at the gate, I got the nerve to ask Doug his opinion.

"Well," he spoke softly, then glanced up at the sky. "She's been gone a day. The Rockies aren't sophisticated. They're upstarts. The other times they've killed it's been in shoot-outs, drive-bys, and robberies. They leave bodies out in the open, front and center."

"So what do you think?"

"Best-case scenario?"

"Please."

"I think they've got Butter and don't quite know what to do. I think they're trying to scare her to make sure she keeps her mouth shut. They won't kill her unless they really have to."

Doug's words of hope were like drops of water. I lapped them up with a parched and guilty conscience as I leaned back against the gate. My chin dropped forward.

"Hey," Doug said, moving in close and leaning against the gate with me. "None of that."

I couldn't say a word.

"Georgia, look at me."

Our eyes met and we exchanged an urgent look.

"I know what you're feeling right now but you can't blame yourself for what's happened. Georgia, you weren't trying to put that little girl in jeopardy. There's no way you could have known it would turn out like this. How could you? I've only known you a little while but my gut tells me that you're careful and you're compassionate."

Then why was I guilt-tripping so hard? Doug's firm and soothing words crept inside my soul and warmed it. Drawn to him, I reached out and touched his forearm. He gave me a reassuring smile. Now Zeke was walking toward us carrying his gear but before we drew apart Doug stroked my back and said gallantly, "C'mon, let's go inside and tackle this thing together."

We walked to the door and rang the bell. I was surprised when a minister—a pudgy, gray-skinned man—answered. He had an engaging smile and his large, pointy ears shifted hard each time he flashed that smile. Black freckles lined his forehead, too. He had on a white short-sleeve shirt with jagged perspiration stains on the collar and underarms. A silver crucifix caught the glimmers of sunlight that came in through the open doorway behind us.

"Ms. Barnett, please come in." His voice had that preachy, deep, it's-baptizing-time tone. "I'm Reverend Kyle Walker. The family asked me to come."

They were probably crazy with worry and needed to feel that some kind of higher power was working for them. I hoped it was, for Butter's sake. And mine.

Four big oval fans stood in each corner blowing into the living room. The connecting rooms were blocked off at the doorways by heavy coal-gray blankets tacked onto the beams. The blankets absorbed the heat but they also killed nearly all of the sunlight in the room.

"This is the Stewart family." Reverend Walker motioned with outstretched arms.

It was so dark I had to squint to see where he was directing us. Butter's family was sitting quietly on the couch. Calling it a couch is giving this piece of furniture the benefit of the doubt. It was really a small love seat missing an arm and butted up against the wall to keep it from falling over.

There was a plump elderly woman, clutching a Bible, with hair as white as washing powder, pressed, oiled, and pulled all the way back in a neat bun. She didn't wear any makeup or jewelry and she had on a blue-and-white-striped cotton pullover dress. She wore fuzzy terry-cloth house slippers with the toes out and beige knee-highs rolled down around her ankles.

Next to her was a young woman with the same high cheekbones and thick eyebrows, but she was rail-thin with splotchy skin decorated with dark spots and healed-over places. Strands of hair were sticking up here and there, air from the fans trying to comb them into place. She was smoking a narrow cigarette but holding it like a joint, taking deep, burdened-by-the-world pulls off the tobacco. Druggie, I thought.

Then there was a little boy about nine or ten sitting on the floor between the legs of the old lady and the druggie. He had his right arm wrapped loosely around the old lady's left leg and he stroked her toes lovingly, all the while looking at me with big experienced eyes. He was a cute kid, slim like the rest of his family, keen-featured, smooth-skinned, wearing a blue T-shirt and shorts with a pair of new Nike gym shoes. He had bandages on his right hand and one on his left knee.

I looked at the two women. Could one of them be the woman I had talked to on the phone? I just didn't think so. I felt no connection to them. Neither spoke; so above all else the aggressiveness of the woman I had talked to was immediately missing.

Then I heard a toilet flush and the snap of a turning door latch. A short woman in her early twenties came out of the rear bathroom. She was using the flat of her palms to adjust the two-piece blue shorts set she had on. Her narrow smooth-skinned face was fair; she had long skinny braids down her back, and she had large bloodshot eyes. She looked dead at me and I got the vibe.

"Kelly?" I asked.

Reverend Walker answered, "Yes, this is the worried mother. May we all be seated."

Now I respect the church but I hoped Reverend Walker wasn't going to get in the middle of this too much. We would need his prayers, but Doug and I

would also need a free flow of communication between us and the Stewarts. It was obvious that he had
prepped the family, the way he had them all sitting
around like they were waiting for a prayer meeting to
start. I looked at my companions. Zeke dropped his
eyes. Doug hunched his shoulders and then introduced himself. "And of course you know reporter
Georgia Barnett."

"Yep!" The little boy smiled at me. Then he said
to the druggie, "She the one put us on TV, Ma."

Butter's mother made the formal introductions
after she moved to sit down on the ottoman at her
mother's side. "Hi, I'm Kelly, and this is my mama,
Miss Mabel. That's my sister, Angel, and her son,
Roger."

"Roger!" The little boy made a loud fart sound
through a slender gap in his front teeth. "My name is
Trip!"

I smiled at him. "Why do they call you Trip?"

Kelly, Angel, Miss Mabel, and the Reverend, all
of them answered at once: "'Cause he always
falling!"

That made everyone laugh.

"Trip, young man," Doug began to ask between
chuckles. "Get us some chairs, huh?"

Trip rolled his eyes.

Miss Mabel snapped, "Boy, if you don't get a
move on, you'd better!"

Trip scrambled up, ran behind one of the blankets, and came back hustling with three folding
chairs. Doug grabbed one and opened it for me.
Zeke declined to take a seat but stood the chair up

next to him as he leaned back against the wall. Doug took the third folding chair and sat near Miss Mabel.

While seated I took a long, deep breath and caught Zeke out of the corner of my eye. He pointed down at his camera resting on the floor but I shook my head no. Zeke scowled at me. I thought, I know . . . I know . . . you always roll whether you use it or not, but not yet. A little girl's life was at stake. I asked God to be my guide.

"Kelly," I began, strong and firm in voice, "I asked Detective Eckart to come here this evening with me. That's because, well, we think that Butter is in danger." Now, I sip facts and spew words for a living. But this was the first time that I hated that I was even opening my mouth. I hated hearing my own voice right now because Butter's mother and grandmother looked like they were about to die from worry.

"She missin', yeah-yeah, but can't y'all find her?" Kelly said as she slunk down and sat on the very edge of the ottoman.

Doug leaned forward toward Kelly, "Can we discuss this privately? Just the family?"

Miss Mabel gave Doug a long, hard stare. "That's all that's here—and the Lord."

Reverend Walker released an affirmative sigh.

"Of course, ma'am," Doug quickly agreed before getting right to the point. "We think that Butter might be being held against her will—"

"Kidnapped?" Reverend Walker's eyebrows arched in surprise.

"Who'd wanna kidnap a baby like Butter?" her grandmother asked. "And what fah?"

"She saw the drive-by the other day," Doug answered.

Please, Doug, break it to the family a little easier.

"Butter," Doug explained further, "saw the shooter and basically described him on television."

"Dear God." Reverend Walker gasped. "She's an eyewitness and they know it."

Instantly Miss Mabel and Kelly reached for each other's hands. Kelly said softly, "Oh Mama."

Angel cursed under her breath, her right hand balled up an empty cigarette package, and she slung it across the room. Kelly was breathing heavily when her eyes met mine. "Is that what caused all this mess? Butter being on TV?"

"It was a mistake to put her on, but I had no idea—"

"Bullshit!" Angel shouted. "It's your fault. You shoulda known better than to put a baby on TV talking about a gangbanger!"

I held my head up, but I felt very bad. What could I say? I'm sorry? I'd jump down my own throat for making a lame remark like that. So I apologized in my heart and explained from my head. "It was not intentional and I'm here to do whatever I can to help—I wanted to help even before I realized who Butter actually was."

"That's right," Zeke spoke up for the first time, trying to have my back. "Georgia fought for the story all day from the minute you called. We only figured out the connection a few minutes ago back at the police station."

"It's still her bad!" Angel snapped, smashing her cigarette butt against the top of a can of cream soda.

"Angel!" Kelly said, grabbing the end seams of her shorts. "Just shut your smart mouth up, okay?!"

"Who you? You don't run me!"

"Listen here!" Miss Mabel shouted.

"Everybody cool down, *now!*" Doug took charge. "This is not the time for fighting or blaming"—he leaned forward—"it's about getting Butter back safe and unharmed."

"Oh my God!" Miss Mabel whispered. It finally really hit her. She closed her eyes. "Y'all have to do something!"

"Are they gonna hurt my baby?" Kelly asked, clenching her fist as her face quickly paled.

"No," I blurted out. Could I will it so? A good reporter follows instinct. I had that and then some. I was born with a caul, what the old folks in the South call a veil. Sometimes . . . sometimes . . . I could feel things. I knew Butter was alive, for some reason, although mainly the reasons that Doug had explained to me earlier. "Tell them, Doug."

"We believe Butter is alive. The Rockies—"

"They better not hurt my grandbaby!" Miss Mabel hissed, sweat beading across her forehead.

"—they aren't going to kill her. They're just trying to scare her and let things cool off until they get the shooter out of town. That's it."

"We must get the word out to the public,"

Reverend Walker said, leaning forward, pointing. "Let those thugs know that we want Butter back and safe."

"No, that's just what we're *not* going to do," Doug countered.

Huh? What's Mister-man thinking? Everyone in the room was surprised, including me. I had assumed that we were going to pump up this story and aim it dead at the Rockies. I waited, we all waited, for Doug's reasoning.

"We don't want to rattle them, make them do something rash. If we put a story on about Butter being kidnapped by the Rockies they might get nervous and do something stupid."

"So how do you want me to handle the story?"

"You just do a straight missing child story, drop the gang references and that will keep the Rockies off-balance and buy our guys enough time to hit the streets."

Everyone seemed okay with the idea except Reverend Walker. He bugged out. "That's no way to deal with these thugs! You've gotta go at them. Subtle is nowhere in their vocabulary. They need fear—fear of what will happen to them if they hurt that child. Force to force is all they understand."

"Mama, Reverend Walker is right." Angel jumped in. "The cops don't really care no'way!"

Doug slowly turned his stare toward Angel. It was the dirtiest, most hateful look I've seen in a long time. Angel was an angry person, combative. She didn't punk out under Doug's stare. I could really feel an edge to this woman. And that fact was working my last nerve. I was about tired of Miss Angel already.

"Officer." Miss Mabel drew Doug's eyes toward her. They instantly filled with sympathy. "I feel like you care. We've got to be careful for Butter's sake because these gangboys are low-down as can be."

"We have to have control of the situation," Doug spoke gently to Miss Mabel and Kelly. "I don't want anything to happen to Butter. Who would want that? No one. From my gut, I'm telling you this is the way to handle the situation."

Quiet became the new person in the room. I looked up at Zeke, who tapped his watch with his pinky finger. Yeah, we had to get rolling—shooting, interviewing, all that for our ten o'clock package. I decided to muscle it.

"I've said that I will do all that I can to help. But all of us in this room know that we have to work together to get Butter back. I say we try Detective Eckart's way because I can always turn my coverage up a notch but you can't tone it down. Still, Butter is your little girl so it's your call."

Kelly looked at me, then Doug, and nodded. Reverend Walker got up and fanned himself with the open palms of his gnarled hands. "Well, I'm no longer needed. I'll call you later, Miss Mabel."

"Reverend, don't leave." Miss Mabel reached out to him.

He simply clutched her hands before walking out. The Reverend was mad. But what could we do? It wasn't time for egos right now.

Kelly pulled out a bulky photo album and showed me pictures of Butter. There was the first-grade class photo—being tall she was standing in the second row. Kelly had a picture of Butter at age three on Santa's lap at the Montgomery Ward store at Evergreen Plaza Shopping Center.

I went to the bedroom Butter and Trip shared. On Butter's side were certificates taped to the wall: perfect attendance, spelling contest second place, and good conduct. Trip pulled out a VCR tape that the family had—Miss Mabel had won a video recorder in the church raffle but eventually sold it when they ran short of money one month.

The picture was fuzzy, the audio scratchy, but there was Butter reciting Dr. King's "I Have a Dream" speech for Sunday school. She had on the same pink and white cotton dress, but it was new.

Then the tape blurred and there was Butter again, the dress more worn and slightly shorter, as she stood in the school auditorium for the spelling bee crying after missing the word *aquarium*.

Then the shot panned away to the crowd, the tape stopped, and there was Butter on the stage holding a certificate and wearing a big T-shirt she'd just won. It was black with white letters, BE #1. It fit Butter like a formal gown. She looked so cute, I thought. Look at that baby!

Then there was another bad spot in the tape, and then there was Butter, same pink dress with the sleeves removed and the hem let out, playing outside. She was dodging in and out of a spray of water from the corner fire hydrant. Butter couldn't help but smile as Trip sprayed her flush in the face and she fell, bouncing off a wave of water on the street, full of laughter.

Zeke was shooting the family watching the home video, then he shot the home video as it played on the television. I talked to Kelly, Trip, and Miss Mabel. Angel agreed with Reverend Walker's position and refused to be interviewed, which was more than fine with me. I didn't want to deal with her 'tude right now.

Doug briefed the family again on how he wanted to handle Butter's disappearance then asked me to walk with him to the door. We promised to share any information we got on the case. Then Doug handed me a card with his home phone number on the back. "Use it, Georgia, if you need to."

I took the card and handed him mine, which also had my home phone number on the back, and said, "You do the same."

After Doug left, I got on the case. I got busy writing my story. Zeke and I went back to the truck and set up a signal; we fed all the tape we'd shot and my voice track back to the studio to be edited together. I was ready to go live.

Standing outside the house, I began to concentrate. I gave a mike check then refused the IFB earplug and told Zeke, "You cue me." He set up a monitor at my feet so I could watch my package on television just as the people at home were seeing it.

Zeke cued me: "Three, two, and . . . Go!"

"I'm Georgia Barnett, live outside of the Stewart

house on the South Side. Inside, the family is distraught and anxious as each member deals with the disappearance of a six-year-old girl named Kelly whom everyone here calls 'Butter.'"

Back at the studio they hit the tape and I watched on the monitor. The piece opened with the home video of Butter.

"I have a dream today," Butter said, smiling, her hands motioning out to the audience.

My voice track came in over the picture: "Butter stole the show at the Sunday school program last year."

Then cut to a wide shot of the Stewart family watching the home video in their living room today.

"The Stewart family is crying, not because the speech itself is so emotional but because for the first time they are watching it without Butter. Butter, you see, is missing."

A sound bite of Kelly popped up as she wiped away tears. "I don't know where she is but all I want is Butter to be back home, where she b'long."

Cut to video of the certificates on the wall. "Butter is a good student who has won these awards for academics and perfect attendance."

Cut to a montage of photos of Butter at school and in the family's backyard during a picnic.

"Family members say Butter is a smart little girl who would never cause trouble for anyone."

A sound bite from Miss Mabel: "Butter is as sweet as can be. And she don't bother nobody and shouldn't no one wanna hurt her."

Video of Butter playing outside by the fire hydrant.

"Friends and neighbors say they last saw Butter playing outside yesterday evening."

The tape froze on a tight shot of Butter smiling and it flew up in the corner revealing a blue full-screen background with the heading, MISSING GIRL.

"Butter is four feet tall and weighs sixty pounds."

The information rippled out in white type against the blue background.

"She is light complexioned with brown eyes and brown hair worn in tiny braids. Butter was last seen wearing a pink and white cotton dress."

Cut to a sound bite of Trip in which I asked him, "Are you worried about Butter?"

"Yeah, Butter don't know how ta look after herself on the street like me."

Cut to a slow push shot into the chalk message on the sidewalk, *Butter Where Are U?* Trip's voice comes up sound full under the picture: "Butter, we miss you. Come home."

Dump tape. Come back to me live at the scene.

"Police have the description of Butter and squad cars in the area are on the lookout for her during their regular patrols. Meanwhile, the family here will wait, wonder, and hope that Butter will soon be back with them safe and sound. I'm Georgia Barnett, live at Fiftieth and South Hedge, back to you in the studio."

Details at Ten

* * *

That was the hardest live shot I'd ever done. After seeing all the pictures, talking to the family, and watching the home video of Butter, I was moved. Now I know her by heart.

SEVEN

*T*he shrill ring of the phone filled my apartment. *Can a sister get some Z's?* I've only been in bed for a couple of hours! The phone rang again. That's when I got scared and mad: scared because anytime the phone rings in the middle of the night it's some serious drama—and mad because the caller was about to drag me dead into it.

"You want her?" the caller asked.

Because the voice was foreign to me, the immune system my body has developed against danger immediately detected trouble. You want her? The meaning of the words scrambled inside my head, which felt heavy on my shoulders. My mind and my body were like a couple dancing off beat. I struggled to get myself together. I tried to focus my burning eyes directly on the clock as I turned it around on my nightstand but I couldn't see a thing.

"Hey, ain't this the TV lady?" the voice questioned in a low hint above a whisper.

"Yes, this is Georgia Barnett. Who is this?" My mind was starting to clear somewhat.

"You want Butter or not?" the voice asked again. It was male, deep, and gruff.

"Yes! Yes!" I said, sitting up, cradling the phone tightly against my ear. "Where is she?"

"Two G's and I'll tell you where."

"Two thousand dollars?"

"Fuck it then!"

"Wait!! When? How?"

"Right now."

"Now?"

Where was I going to get two thousand dollars from now? I asked him this in a calm voice because I did not want to make this guy mad and have him hang up on me. Also, I needed to stall. If I could get him to give me a few hours I could call the police, call Doug, and we could plan this thing out. "I can't get it right now, but later this morning when the banks open I can have it—"

"I ain't stupid! Now, if you wanna know where Butter at, take your ass to one of them cash stations. TV lady like you oughta have plenty of bank!"

He seemed insulted and turned that insult into volume as he shouted the words at me. This guy was no dummy. And I got the feeling that I was making him a dash p-o'ed.

"I have a cash station card but the max out is five hundred dollars in a twenty-four-hour period."

"Five hun'ed ain't shit. I want a grand, ain't takin' less than a grand."

I had some emergency money in my secret stash. I wasn't going to argue another second. "How can I get it to you?"

"Meet me. Where you live?"

Yeah, right, I'm Boo-Boo the Fool; like I was going to tell him my address. "South Shore," I answered.

"Meet me in a half hour, you with this ain't you?"

"Yes, just don't hurt Butter, okay? Where is she?" I began rattling off questions, forcing him to talk longer so that I could tape his voice into my memory. It would be the only thing I would have to recognize him by. I checked my clock. It read 4:00 A.M.

"She aw'ight! Meet me in half an hour—"

"I need at least an hour . . . to get dressed, to get the money . . . to drive where I need to go."

I heard him using his breath to give hard punctuation to a string of dirty words.

He needed a mother like mine; she would truly do something about that nasty mouth of his.

"Slow-ass females! Okay. One hour from now. Bring the money in a brown paper bag to Sixty-second and Calumet. There's a railroad yard under the tracks. Go to the middle where there's a stack of red bricks. You can pull back the fence, it's cut right there, squeeze on through and wait by the third pole. And no five-oh. Five-oh roll up, I roll out."

"Okay, but how will I know you?"

He had already hung up.

I slammed the phone down, jumped out of bed,

went to my dresser, and grabbed Doug's card. I came back to the phone and quickly dialed his number. It rang and rang. *C'mon, Doug, wake up!*

Then the answering machine picked up and Barry White's sensual "Your Sweetness Is My Weakness" began playing in the background. Doug's voice said, "You've got the right number at the wrong time but at the sound of the beep, tell me everything . . ."

Doug had a little mack daddy thing happening on his answering machine and I hesitated. Where is he? Out with a girlfriend? Maybe she's there now and Doug's not picking up?

I heard the beep.

"Ummm," I said, "Doug, this is Georgia. I need your help. I got a call from some guy who says he knows where Butter is. He wants me to meet him at Sixty-second and Calumet, at a rail yard there in an hour and he said no police. I'm afraid to trust anyone else—"

The answering machine clicked off.

I slammed down the receiver, then started to dial the police, but I heard the mysterious voice in my head: *Five-oh roll up, I roll out.* So I hung up the phone. I didn't want to gamble on just any cop. If they made a mistake, Butter might end up dead. Time was ticking away.

A memory flashed through my mind, a memory from long ago. Once, when I had been walking home with my best friend in high school, a man had jumped out from behind a garbage can and grabbed her. I had simply frozen. If a car hadn't scared him off, there's no telling what might have happened.

Fear had made me helpless and angry. From that day on, I promised myself that I'd never back away from trouble, that I'd always fight it. That's the kind of situation I was finding myself in now.

It was dangerous but I had to go by myself and hope Doug would make it there in time to help me. I started to get dressed, grabbing first my jeans, then a T-shirt. I slipped on one shoe and hopped around looking for the other. I found my pager and clipped it onto my belt.

I have a two-bedroom apartment in South Shore, overlooking Lake Michigan and the South Shore Country Club where there are a lot of activities for African Americans. Golfing. Tennis. Plays. Concerts. Poetry readings. Things like that. Usually I glance out of the window and the ornate building will look like a huge boat floating on the lake's waters. When I ran out of my bedroom and through my living room after the call, I could barely make out the outline of the building, let alone the subtle movement of the waves. It was lead black outside and not a star sparkling.

I started playing over the pictures of Butter in my head. The school photos, the home video, and her voice saying, "I have a dream today . . ."

Kidnapped.

The idea grew in my mind like a tornado building at yard's edge, splintering fences and trees that were supposed to protect my innermost property from harm. I had spent most of the night tossing and turning because I was worrying about Butter, a little girl alone among strangers who meant her no good. For hours, several questions had whirled around inside of my head.

Where was Butter? Were they treating her well? Was she crying? Where was she sleeping tonight? How fast could we find her and get her back home?

I took the elevator eight floors down and walked out the front door. The pyramid-shaped wall clock in the lobby said 4:15 A.M. I cleared the revolving door and went to my designated parking spot at the rear of the building. I got in my car—a BMW picked because I want a Black Man Working in my life at all times. I cranked the engine and peeled out.

While driving, I decided that getting money from the cash station was a bad idea, remembering the stories that I'd done on folks who'd gotten killed at night withdrawing money from cash machines. So instead I drove to a twenty-four-hour currency exchange on Stony Island.

This particular currency exchange was frequently used by South Siders. It was bordered on all sides by big, well-traveled streets and located smack-dab on a well-lit corner. This was the safest currency exchange I could find at this time of the morning. I gave my Visa Gold card to the cashier in the cage after filling out a form for a cash advance of $1,000. My nerves were getting more and more edgy as I thought about the task that lay ahead of me.

"How would you like it?" the cashier asked, opening a drawer full of crisp new bills.

An idea suddenly blossomed. "I'd like hundred-dollar bills, please."

I took the money and stuck it in my purse. Now all I needed was the paper bag. There was a gas station a couple of blocks down. It was a handy excuse to feed my sweet tooth. The cashier put my Snickers bar and my can of Diet Dr Pepper in a paper bag. I ran back over to my car and threw the candy bar on the seat, snapped the top on the pop, sipped some, and stuffed the money in the brown bag.

I had to go. And I had to follow the instructions I was given to the letter. A mistake could cost Butter her life. Now who could live with something like that?

EIGHT

I was hyped up . . . and I was alone.

When I checked the clock in my dashboard it read 4:48 A.M., twelve minutes to get to where I needed to be. Finally I pulled my car into the vacant lot of an abandoned hotel. The sound of the engine had been good company and I missed it when I parked. Glimpsing a cop car in my rearview mirror, I quickly ducked down and waited for it to pass. I sat back up and that little voice in my head, that little voice like everyone has, started singing. It was a new song. The verse went: *I don't like this . . . uh-un . . . This is scary.* That was the verse. The chorus went: *You must be crazy, yeah, you must be crazy.*

I took the crisp hundred-dollar bills out of the bag, opened my glove compartment, and took out a bottle of pearl white fingernail polish I kept there.

Flipping the bills over, in the part where it says "In God we trust" I whited out the word *In* with the polish. I was dotting, blowing, and fanning the bills to dry them. I checked my watch and the clock in the dash and realized I had somewhere shy of five minutes left. Quickly, I gathered the bills back together, folded five of them, and put them into the paper bag. The other five I folded and palmed in my hand.

It was a short walk over to the third pole by the tracks. I could see it through the darkness in the distance. My steps were steady, firm, maybe even sure as I began my sojourn to meet the voice that I'd hoped would whisper to me the secret of Butter's whereabouts. Although it was dark and spooky, fear did not overwhelm me. I thought of my sister, Peaches, who always says I'm stone crazy with a dash and a half of nerve.

I stopped walking when I saw a stack of red bricks behind the fence. The fence was tall, silver, with spiked wire loops coiled across the top. Nearing the third pole, I reached down and tugged at the fence and part of it peeled back just as my instructions said. Boyfriend didn't lie. Turning sideways, I squeezed through and walked over to the third pole, then tagged it with my hand. I thought, okay now you're it.

The pole was just inches from the overhead el tracks. There was nothing beneath the tracks but trash, the lame leg of a table . . . the carcass of a compact car . . . wild weeds . . . raggedy iron rails . . . speckles of shattered glass . . . and the smell of stale pee. Nice way to start a morning, huh?

Suddenly the night's sounds were interrupted by

the caller. I heard the same voice I'd spoken with earlier on the phone. "You got it?" My head snapped in the direction of the voice, which was coming from behind a green metal switch box about fifteen feet away.

I squinted and answered, "Yes."

I couldn't see squat. The guy's body was hidden by the box. It was about eight feet high and three feet wide. I just saw the black toes of his sneakers, one foot flat on the ground and the other foot cradled leisurely on top of a rock.

"It's so dark out here," I said.

"You can't be afraid of the dark?! Better not be. Night never ends, baby," he replied, then laughed a bit. "Just toss me the money."

"How do I know you're not trying to rip me off? Huh? You might not know where Butter is!" My mama ain't raise no pushover. I'd come this far and I wasn't about to just roll over and play stupid.

I saw the toes of his shoes as his feet shifted. Two seconds later something came flying at me. I dodged and it hit off the pole, landing at my feet. It was a piece of material, pink and white cotton, wrapped around a rock with a rubber band—a piece of Butter's dress!

"Now, toss the money here!"

I put the rock in the bag, wrapped the rubber band around it, and threw the bag back like I was trying to go upside his head with it. Instead a long arm reached out and caught it in midair, snatching the bag behind the metal box that continued to shield his body.

"Where's Butter?"

"Where's tha rest at?" he shouted back, crunching the paper bag with a pop. "This just half!"

"I've got it here. Tell me where she is and I'll give you the rest."

"Why you fucking playing? Give me the rest of the money, then I'll tell you."

As I walked closer, clutching the cloth, in the distance I heard the faint rumble of the el train moving our way. Everything was coming to me exceptionally loud and exceptionally clear. The train sound was grrrrr-clack. Grrrrr-clack.

Just as the train turned the bend and came barreling overhead, the beat kicked up a notch: GRRRRR-CLACK-CLACK! I bent my knees to drop the money and . . . something moved. Then glass broke somewhere nearby and I jerked around, shifting my body in that direction. I glimpsed a scrawny, gold-colored cat jetting away in the darkness.

"Bitch, you done brought somebody!" the caller shouted and I heard his steps coming toward me hard and fast.

"No," I shouted. But before I could turn my head to look him in the eye, he grabbed me and slammed me back against the metal box. My shoulder took the brunt of the blow, making me bounce off the structure and hit the ground. He was on me now, pushing my face down. "Gimme the money!"

I felt the dirt against my cheek, and my nose filled up with the musky smell of neglected, abused soil. My purse was out in front of me after flying off my shoulder. I landed on my other arm, pinning the money beneath me. I couldn't hear anything but the last sounds of the train passing. Then I felt his hot, sweaty hand on the back of my neck as he squeezed it and shook my body.

With adrenaline and anger pumping through my legs and arms, I jerked with every ounce of strength I had and flipped on my side. He seemed surprised at my strength and that moment of hesitation helped me as I kicked up with my right leg, catching him on the hip. I felt the weight from the kick in my ankle and I grunted as he flipped backward. I looked up but all I could see were sparks like fireworks floating down as the train roared on in the distance. I turned on my side, pushed off with my hands, tried to get up, but slipped backward and then *he was on me again.*

"Gimme! Bitch! Bitch!"

He dissed me in a hateful whisper that gave me more fear and more anger than before.

With all I had, I reached for my Mace, which had rolled out of my purse. He grabbed my arm from behind. His weight pinned me facedown again and he twisted my arm behind my back. I yelled, and mixed with my voice I heard another.

"Police!"

The weight rolled off me; reflex more than anything else made me turn and swipe at him with my arm. I caught the edge of his heel and tripped him up a bit. He started falling forward, but he kept his legs moving and started to windmill his arms, which kept him balanced. Suddenly gunfire erupted in the night and a chill ran through me. Bullets are blind.

My body ain't fat-free but it's bullet-free and I planned on keeping it that way. I covered my head, then peeked out from under my elbow in time to see a shot miss his fleeing heel. Two beat cops were chasing him now, two old guys, they were big-time heavy. Those guys had a better chance of catching the lottery than of catching my mystery man.

Clutching the piece of Butter's dress in my hand, I squeezed it tighter out of frustration. I mean I wanted to jump on somebody! My heart pounded and it was a chore to merely catch my breath.

"Georgia, are you okay?"

I recognized Doug's voice and stretched out my body right there on the ground and moaned, "No-oooooo." In the distance two more shots rang out. I felt Doug's hands around my shoulders as he lifted me up into a sitting position.

Like oil and water, exhaustion and adrenaline do not mix. My head wobbled before falling left to rest against Doug's shoulder as he checked the arm I was cradling gently. My body was moving like the scarecrow in The Wizard of Oz. I closed my eyes and a picture of me at six falling off a set of monkey bars flashed through my mind.

"Let me take a look," Doug said, more to himself than to me, as he carefully examined my forearm.

I struggled to straighten up a bit and Doug held me close. "Lean on me."

It was a great relief to rest and let him help me.

"It's not broken. Does it hurt, Georgia?"

"No, it's just numb from falling on it, I think."

Umphf! My mistake. I bragged on myself too soon. When Doug raised my arm outward, prickly nerves danced beneath my flesh and pain found my elbow. "Awww! Sssssh—take it easy."

"Serves you right, coming out here alone!" Doug scolded now that he realized that my injury was minor. "He could have killed you, you know that?"

"Well, I tried to get help from you," I shot back. "Where were you? Out—" then I stopped before saying, *with some woman?* My face flushed.

Doug waited two long beats before saying, "I was out driving one of my friends home. He's got a drinking problem. His girl called me from a bar because he wouldn't give up the car keys—that is till I got there."

I felt about as big as an extra in The Wizard of Oz. Our eyes met and Doug had a glint in his. He was enjoying the fact that I had been a bit jealous. "It was a boneheaded idea you coming out here by yourself, but all in all, you handled yourself pretty well."

"Thanks, I guess those self-defense classes paid off."

Suddenly our attention was captured by the two cops who were now slowly walking back our way. "Aww, hell," Doug cursed, "they didn't get him!"

Doug began directing the officers. "Okay. Let's check the immediate area and get an evidence tech down here. Georgia, where was he? And where were you?"

Doug helped me up and I pointed out the green switch box, the stack of red bricks, and finally the iron rails. "They've got half the money—five hundred dollars. I marked it."

"How?"

"I asked the cashier at the currency exchange to give me new hundred-dollar bills and I took nail polish and whited out the word *In,* see?" And I showed Doug the bills I had left.

"Nice idea, but you need to leave the police business to me."

I was too tired to crack back. We waited around for the evidence technician who worked this district. A small, wiry man in jeans, a short-sleeved blue shirt, and dark blue tie arrived in about twenty minutes. He had thick, black hair everywhere, on his head, eyebrows, and wisps coming out of his nose. He grunted out the name, Tillner, and asked me to point out all the places where the suspect was standing.

I walked him and Doug over to the metal switch box. Tillner opened up his evidence case and inside were three powders: white, black, and black metallic. He also had an assortment of brushes with soft hair that fanned out like the ones women use to apply makeup.

"Think you'll be able to lift something?" Doug asked.

"I'm the master." Tillner sniffed, then spit as he got on his knees and examined the metal surface of the switch box. "I don't miss jack. The crapshoot comes later. The print I lift has to match a person with a set on file. The computer will spot the match and spit out a suspect."

Doug gently took me by the arm, leading me off

to the side. "Okay, Georgia, think. Did you get a look at the suspect's face at all?"

"No, Doug, he kept holding me down and turning my face away."

"Your mind could be hiding stuff from you. You can't remember anything distinguishable about him?"

I shook my head no.

"Do you remember what he said?"

"On the phone he asked did I want Butter, and he asked for money, and he told me where to be, and I came. He gave me a piece of Butter's dress as proof . . . then the stray cat ran through and all Cain broke loose."

"Okay. You need to come back to the station with me right now. I've got some mug shots for you to look at. Maybe they'll jog your memory."

"Okay."

Doug helped me walk over to my car. "Can you follow me or do you want me to have one of the officers drive your car?"

"I can drive, I'm okay," I said, reaching for the door.

Then I noticed . . .

. . . I noticed it was still in my hand.

I turned around, took Doug's hand, and placed the cloth in his palm. "Butter's dress," I said, and closed his fingers around the cloth.

NINE

___

No . . . No . . . No!" I paused as I scanned Doug's personal scrapbook of mug shots of the gangbangers in his district. "Gangbanging must be the only occupation with no age discrimination."

"Yep. These guys range in age from fourteen to thirty-five. And most of them look like regular guys waiting for the el train."

"Yeah, I guess I was like the average naive citizen thinking they'd look like the wolfman with a fade or a black Hannibal Lecter substituting pintos for fava beans."

"Georgia, they're regular-looking but freak-a-zoid acting. I can tell you some wild stories."

"That's quite all right. That's more info than I need. None of these men look remotely familiar at all. But ah . . ." I flipped back two pages and stared at a corner photo.

"Got something?"

"No, I just thought he had a really scary look to him—but I don't think that's the guy—he's just a little more menacing than the others. There's something funky about him."

Doug pulled out a folder with a Polaroid stapled to the top left-hand corner. He purposely held it close to his stomach to block out the address and other critical info. "Here's a better picture. That's Little Cap. The shooter in the drive-by."

Little Cap's eyes were oval platters of hazel; without the anger and defiance, they could be sweet love windows for a woman to gaze into. He had ruddy lacquered skin, an awning of black eyebrows, evenly spaced features, and a long, hard chin. A scar could be seen turning the corner on the left side of that chin, ending at a round, flat mole. It looked like someone had cut an exclamation point in his face.

"Little Cap has priors dating back to the age of fourteen. He's twenty-three years old now. He's fairly high in the Rockies organization," Doug explained. "He's often called on to do the dirty work."

"Yeah, he looks like he could do some damage."

Suddenly the door opened. Doug put the folder down on the desk and had a mini-conference with another detective at the door. Doug's back was to me, and I couldn't see the face of the detective he was talking to, just hear the smothered whispers of their voices.

Finally Doug shut the door, turned around, and came back over to me. "We've been rattling every sewer top on the South Side looking for this snake. Little Cap is in hiding, waiting for the heat to go down on the drive-by."

"I hope he's stupid enough to get homesick and turn up in the wrong place. Then maybe some snitch will turn his raggedy butt in," I snorted.

"Not likely. He's always been a vagabond, not many friends or very trusting, even within the gang. Little Cap always bounces around here and there for just a minute—his family claims they haven't seen him in a year. Naw, Little Cap wouldn't be under the el trying to put the squeeze on you. He wouldn't take a chance like that. If anything, he'd send one of the other bangers out. I just wanted you to see him though, get a good look at what we're dealing with."

"What time is it?" My sleep jones was coming down hard on me.

"Early," Doug said as he turned the page for me. Then he stood up, backpedaled to the door, opened it, and called out, "Ray, get us two black coffees huh?"

"Three sugars," I said.

"Heavy sugar," Doug ordered. "Georgia, you get back to those books. It's important."

I looked up at Doug. "You don't have to sell me; I know."

His eyebrows raised.

"Nope," I answered the question only his eyes asked. "I wasn't the victim of a crime. But I did witness one when I was a kid. Some nut grabbed my friend and tried to pull her into an alley. Luckily she was able to break away, but she was so hysterical she couldn't give a description of the guy. I could."

"Good enough for a sketch?" Doug asked as he sat on the edge of the desk, one foot swinging free and the other nestled toe first in a warped pocket on the floor.

"Yep, someone saw it on the news, phoned in a tip, and the police put the guy away."

"That's what I'm talking about—more people have to step up and help us, get involved."

"Well, I'm certainly involved now, that's for sure. I've got kidnappers calling my crib in the wee hours of the morning!"

"Speaking of, we're putting a trace on that call to your apartment. Hopefully we'll come up with something soon, Georgia."

The door opened and Ray came in with a gray paper beverage container. One hole was empty, the others held long white cups of coffee and he had a newspaper rolled up under his arm. He sat the container on the table, picked up one of the cups, and sipped it. "Well," Ray said, savoring the jolt of caffeine, "there's good news and bad news."

Doug and I both looked up at him.

"The good news is that the coffee is good. The bad news is this!" And Ray opened the Chicago Defender newspaper and tossed it on the table before walking back out the door.

You could have knocked me out with a paper wad.

The headline: GANG KIDNAPS GIRL.

Below the headline was a big picture of Butter, one of those I had seen in the Stewart family scrapbook.

"Dammit!" Doug cursed.

I started reading the copy to Doug:

"'In a neighborhood plagued by gang violence, yet another offensive act has occurred that clearly points to chaos in the inner-city community. A six-year-old girl named Kelly Johnson is missing. Affectionately known to friends and family as Butter, the little girl is believed to have been kidnapped by the Rockies, a neighborhood street gang. . . .'"

"I specifically told them to keep a lid on this thing." Doug moaned.

"Obviously they ain't scared of you!" I cracked.

Doug picked up the copy where I left off: "'Butter's family says she witnessed a drive-by shooting in the neighborhood two days ago. Five people were shot and one victim remains hospitalized in critical condition. Butter was interviewed by television reporter Georgia Barnett of Channel 8 News. . . .'"

"Oh, that's low-down!"

Doug cracked a smile. "Obviously they ain't scared of you either!"

This bad pub would linger on me like funk after a two-hour workout.

"Don't worry about it." Doug shrugged.

"Don't worry about it? They just busted me out! Black folks read the Defender like crazy! And all the television stations in town get it and scan it for stories, too. I'm getting dogged-out in front of my people and my peers."

"Your temper's showing," Doug said with a slight smile.

I know it is, dap-gum-it! I took the paper back and started reading again. "'. . . In Barnett's live broadcast, Butter gave a sketchy description of one of the suspects, but vivid enough, police think, to prompt gang members to kidnap her. In an exclusive interview, Reverend Kyle Walker railed against what he called an incompetent Chicago Police Department. . . .' "

"Incompetent?!" Doug shouted. "Who is that Al Sharpton wanna-be calling incompetent?"

"Uh-un, practice what you preach: *temper, temper!*"

"Gimme here!" Doug said, grabbing the paper back, and snapping it.

I laughed, "'Gimme here'?"

Doug read, "'. . . what he called an incompetent Chicago Police Department for delaying to search for the little girl. 'The police don't care about a little black child in the ghetto, but we do,' Reverend Walker said. 'We love Butter and want to tell those gangbangers to bring her back unharmed! We're fed up and revved up.' '"

"People kill me," I said.

"No, we need to kill some people. Like this newspaper reporter. Like Reverend Walker . . ."

"Like those knuckleheads who run my shop," I groaned, looking at my pager, which had just gone off. "The station is paging me now. I need to call in."

I reached for the phone, but Doug pulled it away from me. "Listen, that little adventure you had this morning? I need you to sit on that information. I'll make sure it stays quiet on this end. This thing is already out of control."

"Doug, why on earth would I sit on the sole exclusive fact that I have right now? The Right Reverend has blown up the story. Keep quiet on my end? You've got to be kidding me."

"Georgia, I'm working on more things than you know and I can't tell you about them. But I need you to keep your ransom episode under wraps. You do right by me with this, I'll keep you deep in the loop. Besides, you don't want every nut and faker calling our headquarters and your station with phony leads and ransom demands, do you?"

"Of course not, but—"

"But nothing, Georgia. Every nut with a cell phone hookup will be dialing us. We'll get swamped and distracted from the real goal, which is to find Butter. Work with me. And I need you to finish going through these books."

I sat there and thought, if I called in, they'd want me to come into the station right away.

"What's on your mind, Georgia?"

"Well, Doug, I'm nightside, which means I'm due in at one o'clock this afternoon and I work through the ten o'clock show. It's eight now. The morning crew is there and the managers told the desk to page me now. So, I know they want me to work a double—come in now and work straight through until the ten. But I wanna follow you right now and see what you're going to do next on this thing. I've got a change of clothes in my trunk that I keep in case I get sent out of town on a story; I can finish going through these pictures, change somewhere, and have the crew pick me up here and we'll trail you—"

"No!"

"Doug! You're tying my hands on everything. I'm working with you but you're not working with me!!"

"I can't have a camera crew traipsing around with me. It's bad enough with just you. People freak out and start acting crazy when you turn a TV camera on them. Now tell me they don't, huh?"

"Awwwww, Doug-Doug, this Butter kidnapping has got me tripping out. Can't you see that?"

"I know. That's why I'm letting you in on so much. I know you feel it's your fault. But you have to trust me that I know what's best to find Butter."

My pager went off again. I checked the number. It was the station again.

"It's on you," Doug said, picking up the phone and plopping it down in front of me. "Can you stay and finish looking at these mug shots? I'll owe you big time."

TEN

Doug did owe me big time; one, because I stayed an extra hour and a half scrutinizing mug shots with no luck. And two, because I fully intended to sit on this morning's ransom incident as asked. But I wonder if boyfriend knew that I was going to call in that chip five minutes after I stepped out of the cop shop?

I don't think so.

Doug wasn't going to like it. But he was just going to have to lump it.

Simply put, Doug owed me and I had a hunch.

A good reporter has a built-in hunch factor. That hunch factor is an unknown variable, like X. What was my hunch?

Well, it started with Doug.

He'd tried very hard to keep Little Cap's file close to the vest. But when he went to the door, I sneaked a peek because all is fair in love, war, and reporting. I saw and memorized Little Cap's real name and last known address, which just happened to be with his mother, Audrey Darrington.

As sure as I know that my birth certificate says "Negro," I knew that Doug had already questioned Little Cap's mother until she couldn't think straight. But I wanted to talk to her. I needed to get a better feel for Little Cap.

No person is born a criminal. A person is exposed to negative influences that create criminal behavior.

What was Little Cap like growing up? Did he do well in school? Who grew up in the house with him? His mother and father? Sisters and brothers? What were his friends and neighbors like?

I went to investigate and found myself standing on the porch of an old brick Georgian house bordered by a trashy vacant lot and a well-kept community garden. Collards, tomatoes, and hot peppers were being carefully watered by an elderly man. Children busily played their way up and down the street on bikes, skates, and by foot as I rang the bell at Alexander Darrington's, aka Little Cap's, house.

I didn't call for a crew, partly because I was hiding until my shift started and partly because I didn't want to spook the family into not talking to me.

A tall woman, nearly six feet, with signs of age from deep wrinkles to streaks of gray, opened the door and stared hard at me. She had neat, tight locks styled away from her face, down her back. She wore a V-neck cotton dress, teal green, with short sleeves. Dark lids shaded her listless hazel eyes. She asked, "Can I help you?"

"Audrey Darrington, please."

She blinked hard. "She's not—"

"Hi, Audrey. I'm Georgia Barnett with Channel 8—"

Audrey tried to slam the door.

I stuck my foot in it. Size ten. Hard-heeled from summers playing barefoot down South. My foot could brake for a Lincoln Town Car.

"I want to talk to you about Alexander—not Little Cap," I said. "I think you did your best to raise him to be a good boy, to be a good man. We both know he's tied into gangs. I don't know what the police think or said to you. But me? Me, Audrey? I just don't think it's your fault. It's the outside influences that are to blame. It's . . . it's . . . just so bad on these streets."

Audrey jumped in, dabbing her fingertips at the glistening sweat beading on her chest. "And the streets have a vise hold on these boys. What can you do? The streets can just take your child, even if you've got your eye on him—the streets just take your child."

Audrey was looking away now, somewhere in a direction not on my compass but found only on hers.

I let her go there, then I asked easily, "Audrey, may I please come in and talk?"

She looked at me for a moment, then said, "Of course. Where are my manners today?"

The house was cleaner than the Board of Health. No dust. No papers or old magazines lying around.

My mother would praise her to high heaven while kicking me to the curb in hell for the way my place looked most of the time. The furniture in the house was old but well made and solid; that antique-style stuff that you can't find anymore. There was a pink and baby blue porcelain lamp with angels on a merry-go-round on a table right behind the couch where we sat. The rose Jacquard curtains were open and we could see by the sunlight shining through the big picture window just a few feet away. Beneath the picture window sat an open red and white cooler chock-full of ice, with pops, ice cream bars, and juices.

Audrey noticed me checking it out. "I keep that stuff for the kids, when it gets hot every summer. They come to the door every day like it's Halloween and I give them treats until I don't have any more. The orange Popsicles were a favorite of my boy's."

"Alexander?"

"No, Simon, my oldest."

"Is that him with Little Cap there?" I asked, pointing to a picture on the end table behind the curve of her hip.

"Yes." She blinked. "I hate nicknames. Alexander got his nickname because he loved playing with cap guns when he was a little bitty something."

"Of course," I apologized. I pointed to the picture again. "Does Simon live here in Chicago?" My mind was racing as I awaited her answer. Was he a gang member, too? Could he be helping Little Cap and the Rockies hold Butter hostage?

"No, he was killed."

"I'm sorry."

Audrey began to rock slightly. "It hurts like yesterday but it was nearly ten years ago."

"Can you tell me how it happened? Did Alexander take it hard?"

"Take it hard?" Her laugh was loud and bitter. "He was the cause of it."

"How?"

"Simon was a good child. He was an A student and all the teachers loved him. He wanted to go into the service and be one of those Navy Seals. My son was a swimming champion in the public high school league. He was tops in his ROTC class. Alexander idolized his brother and the fight he had in him. Simon was tough but he only fought for what was right and he fought fair. He'd get on Alexander's case when he was wrong, which was often, even in front of the other kids."

"Alexander didn't like that, I'm sure."

"No, he didn't," Audrey said, throwing her head back and then nervously dropping her head forward and lightly clasping her hands together.

"What kind of a person is Alexander?"

"He's quiet. Intense. Ornery. Traits that simmered as he grew older. But after Simon's murder, Alexander got downright mean. I wonder sometimes, truly wonder. I say to myself, God, is that really my child? Lord, did Alexander really come from me?"

Audrey took a long pause.

"Did Alexander and his brother get along?"

She smiled. "Alexander loved him some Simon.

And Simon loved and kept a lid on Alexander."

"You said Simon's death was Alexander's fault."

"One day Alexander went to the store for Simon. Alexander got into a fight with one of the boys on the other side of the park. They came to blows and Alexander got stomped when the boy's friends jumped in the fight."

Audrey stopped rocking and cradled her elbows with the palms of her hands. "I wasn't home, but they tell me Alexander grabbed Simon by the shirt on the porch, shook and begged him to go back with him to keep the others away while he got back at the boy. Why did Simon go? That wasn't like Simon. But Alexander convinced him that it wasn't a fair fight and that he should take up for him like he did all the other kids in the neighborhood. But that damn Alexander had gotten a gun from one of his bad-boy friends and didn't tell Simon. And it turned out that Alexander wasn't the only one with a gun. One of those other boys had a gun, too. Simon was shot and killed right there in that park like a dog."

"What about Alexander?"

"Shot in the leg; still favors it on the right side." Audrey chuckled to herself. "Gave him a cool walk. Don't you know kids around here on both sides of the park try to imitate that walk? Kids are something, aren't they?"

"Has Alexander felt guilty about his brother's death all this time?"

"Yes, he has. It did something to him, that guilt. It turned into a low-down meanness after while. But I feel guilty too. Maybe I didn't help. I should have

99

paid a little more attention to Alexander after his brother died. I was nursing my grief and he just grew up wild. When he got damn near grown and started getting into serious trouble, I let him stay here as long as I could but . . . a Christian person has a conscience and can't tolerate too much wrong even if it is her own child doing it. But I really do believe that Alexander has been fighting and looking for revenge ever since his brother's death."

"Revenge against whom?"

Audrey stood up and walked slowly over to the large picture window, not saying a syllable until she leaned against the wall. "Against the world, himself, me, I think, for loving Simon just a little more."

"I'm curious. Back up a little if you can. What was the fight in the park over? The one that got Simon killed?"

Audrey leaned down and slowly fished out a can. "Over a can of pop." She opened it, took a long sip, then shook her head before looking out the window again.

"You know there's a little girl missing and Alexander and his gang are involved. He could help the police get her back safely. Her mother is worried and the child is only six. Please, Mrs. Darrington, do you know where Alexander is?"

Audrey shook her head no.

"Please," I begged. "I know it's hard to tell—"

"I don't know anything. If I did, I would say just to save that little girl. I know what a mama feels like when her child is gone."

Suddenly a shadow slipped across the right side

of Audrey's face. She turned to the window, and her eyes got wide with fear.

I saw it coming, glass and fire spinning end over end. The hair on the back of my neck prickled.

Audrey screamed. I jumped off the couch and reached for her. The picture window shattered. My hands shot out in front of my face as pin-needles of glass came flying my way.

I heard a boom and a whoosh!

When I uncovered my eyes, Audrey was on the floor, her hands over her head. Broken glass was everywhere and the curtains were blooming with flames. I yelled, "Fire! Fire!" The flames were the tortoise and I was the hare.

I spun on the hardwood floor and kicked over the cooler with my heels. The ice and water gushed out and doused the flames eating at the baseboard.

Audrey was screaming and backing away on the floor. I grabbed a broom standing in the corner and knocked the curtain rod—flames and all—out onto the front porch through the shattered window. The elderly man tending the community garden turned his hose on the porch and the flames gurgled and belched like a thirsty animal.

As the flames died down, I had a panicked thought. Where's Audrey? I spun around and she was cowering in the corner, blood all over her face. A cruising squad car hit the brakes in the middle of the street. One of the police officers jumped out of the vehicle and was now jackknifing through the crowd that stood gaping at the raggedy opening of the picture window.

The police officer asked, "What happened?"

Someone said the car was black.

Someone said it was dark green.

Someone said there were three teenagers in the car.

Someone said it was two teenagers and a kid.

Someone said they yelled "Bandits Rule!"

Someone said they yelled "Motherfuckers!"

Someone said it was an M-80 that was thrown through the window.

Someone else said it was a bunch of firecrackers in a bottle.

The bomb and arson squad got down to the real nitty-gritty. They said it was gasoline in a mayo jar with duct tape around the seal and a greasy rag for a wick.

Apparently the Bandits had tried to get revenge against the Rockies by firebombing Little Cap's mother's house. They had hoped to kill somebody. By the grace of God they hadn't.

Audrey would live, but she would have an ugly scar from the three-inch gash on her forehead. She was trembling when she was put into the ambulance. It took about twenty minutes for Doug to get there. He looked at me with a vicious scowl. "What are you doing here?"

"Selling Mary Kay so I can get a pink Caddy?"

"A smart mouth will get you in bad," he snapped.

My grandmother used to say that.

"Georgia, how'd you find out about Little Cap's mother?"

"I've got sources," I lied. I started to say I'm nosy

and I've got eyes but too much smart mouth really will get you in bad—and I was in enough bad already.

"Don't play me, Georgia. Don't ever fuckin' play me."

"You owed me, Doug," I said, and didn't even blink.

After about five seconds of our stare-down, he relented. "Are you okay?" Doug held his belligerent tone like Patti LaBelle holds that last note on "Somewhere Over the Rainbow."

"Yeah, just tired and shaken up. I gave the other detectives my statement. Things are getting hot, huh?"

"For real."

"Doug, you guys have got to find Butter. Things are getting too hot—they might just decide to . . ."

Doug nodded because he understood far too well.

I used my cell phone to call the station. I had them rush a crew out to shoot the scene. This would be the top to my story tonight at six when I updated Butter's case. I would talk to Butter's family, too, and likely be live from their house. I had the lead story.

Or so I thought.

ELEVEN

I got big-footed—the ultimate insult to a TV news reporter.

After my crew got finished shooting video of the scene and a quick interview, I trailed them back to the station. It was now about 1:00 in the afternoon.

I didn't feel like getting hit flush in the face with some mess so I decided to call one of my girls at the station to see what the buzz was. I knew people were talking about me: one for iging the page this morning and two for being at the house when it was fire-bombed.

Journalists are natural humbuggers. It's the curiosity in them. It's the energy and creativity in them. It's the daily burden of always having to be factual and prompt within seconds for their jobs. Something will happen in a newsroom, something big or small, the taste of it will get in folks' mouths, and, like a bad cold, it spreads from one person to another, almost invisibly, with speed and power and no common cure.

I knew they were dogging me today with all that was going on with this story so I called my friend Clarice, who is a researcher on the assignment desk and always has the scoop. I called her direct line and listened to her cigarette-roughened voice: "Channel 8, we get you the news first!"

"It's me, girl."

"Georgia," she whispered. "Are you okay? I heard about what happened! I was worried to death!"

"It was crazy but I'm fine. I'm on the way in now. Listen, what's going on there at the station?"

"No," Clarice said, cutting me off. "I haven't heard about that organization."

Somebody must be standing around her desk and she couldn't talk. So I did the talking. "Clarice, I got some negative pub in the *Defender* today, plus I blew off a page this morning. I need to know if the do-do is hitting the wind machine or not."

"Well, what I can do is this," she said in her same even-toned voice. "In a few minutes, I'll go back and check my mailbox for your organization's press kit, then I can talk to you at length about whether or not it would be a story our station might cover, how's that?"

That was a little sister secret code we had. That meant that Clarice was going to go float around the newsroom and hear what people were saying about what had happened this morning when I didn't call in. Then Clarice would meet me in the back office where the staff mailboxes and schedules were posted. It was out of the way and had very little traffic.

I entered the building from the rear. I was waiting at our designated meeting spot for less than five minutes when Clarice walked up and said, "Hey, Georgia."

Clarice's physical appearance is juxtaposed with her personality. Her gritty voice and outgoing personality do not match her dainty body. Clarice is a petite person: little hands, little feet, size 6 dress, about five-two, and delicate features. She likes to sit at her desk, legs crossed, leaning forward with her elbows on the desk, poring over some AP wire copy with a cigarette smoldering nearby in some wacky, freebie ashtray that came in the mail. Clarice was working a cigarette butt now.

She said, "Made the paper, huh?"

"I know! I couldn't believe they dogged me like that."

"I think that sometimes print journalists like to take a swipe at broadcast journalists because we pimp so many of their stories. You know how sometimes we let them break the story and then we hop on it later and don't always give them credit. This is just a little payback. I don't think it's personal."

"Yeah, maybe you're right," I said. "It still stings though. But listen, tell me, what'd you hear?"

"Some people talking around the assignment desk were saying that you got beat on the story yesterday—"

"Beat! I did *not* get beat!"

"Ssssh!" Clarice said, taking a long pull off her cigarette before dropping it on the tile floor and putting it out with a twist of the toe. "Do you want someone walking by to hear?"

I lowered my voice but not my rage. "Clarice, I knew that the Rockies had Butter!"

"Well, why didn't you put that in your story?"

"Because Doug asked me not to. He asked the whole family to keep a lid on it because he thought leaking information would make it harder to find Butter! But Reverend Walker didn't cooperate."

"Who is Doug?"

"Doug Eckart. He's the detective working the drive-by and he's also trying to help find Butter."

"Wait a minute! I was helping do some research for a piece about two months ago and I had to go out and interview a cop. He turned out to be a fine brother. He was tall, reddish brown, long lashes, fine eyebrows, and . . . and—"

"That was Doug!"

"Yeah, and as I recall he's single—I didn't see a ring or anything, never mentioned a wife. So after this is over, are y'all going to get a little *thang* going?"

"Don't start."

"C'mon, tell me!"

"Clarice, I'm trying not to put my business in the street."

She grinned. "Well, just think of me as a dead end, it's not going anywhere. C'mon, I'm your girl, remember?"

"Yeah." I smiled. "You are. And yeah I like him.

There's just something about him. He's good-looking, he seems real dedicated, we've been flirting, but so far on the romantic tip there's nothing for certain . . ."

"Yet." Clarice winked at me. "A brother that fine, you've got to be trying to hook up with him, huh?"

"Well, I'm still trying to get over Max, I don't need any drama!"

"Doug could be the break you need! It's not like good-looking, working brothers pop up in a sister's life every day now. I think you should—"

"Clarice, get off that and get down to the gristle. What did they say about me not coming in when I was paged?"

"Well, they started dogging you out, saying that you didn't answer the page because you were embarrassed about getting beat on the story and getting dissed in the paper."

"Who said that?"

"This one and that one. Now what I'm going to tell you next is really going to make you angry. Don't go off, okay?"

"Do I ever go off?"

"Off the deepest of ends and with more regularity than Correctol!"

"Shut up! But . . . I promise."

"Okay. They've big-footed you."

I got big-footed. Big-footed meant that they kicked one reporter off something important and put the person considered the bigger star on the story. "With whom?"

"Brent Manning."

"Those low-down dirty dogs! Brent Manning makes me sick! Everybody in this station knows I can't stand him. They deliberately gave him my story to get on my last nerve."

Brent Manning was one of those guys who thinks he's all that, and while he's good, he's not Scoop the Journalism God. Brent is TV news; the man is cut from network tape. He's lanky, with chiseled features, blue eyes, blond hair, and he's aggressive like nobody's business. He can smell a story a mile away. Brent is doggish about news, too, always criticizing something and somebody because he's a perfectionist. Now he was on my story and getting it back would be like trying to get my arm out of a pit bull's mouth. "Where is Brent now?"

"I heard that he's out going on a ride-along with one of the beat cops in the neighborhood. You know, they've got flyers of this kid and they're supposed to go door-to-door canvassing the neighborhood."

"Thanks, C!" I hugged her and went to my desk.

I was going to go see my boss, Bing. But I kept getting sidetracked. People kept stopping by my desk, asking if I was okay, and riding me about getting dogged in the paper. There was already a Post-it on the computer that said Bing wanted to see me. Some tattletale must have told him I was in, because Bing came right up behind me and noted, "Obviously you're okay. Good."

The crowd around me flew. Bing could clear a room faster than fire. He grunted. "Georgia, my office."

109

We walked to his office in silence. Bing sat at his desk where he had been watching an air-check, which is a recorded copy of a live broadcast. It was a copy of last night's ten o'clock news, currently set on pause.

"Now," Bing said with a dissatisfied look on his face, "your story last night made no mention that this missing kid case is gang related."

Pride wanted me to say I knew. Instinct wanted me to lie. But as my grandmother used to say, pride goeth before a fall. "I had a hint of it but I couldn't confirm it so I didn't go with it. I didn't want to risk being wrong and escalating the gang situation there."

Bing talked about me like a D-O-G. As he ranted and raved I was a silent spectator, stuck and unamused. I waited patiently for him to take a break. "Bing, I heard that you put Brent on this story," I finally managed to get in. "I heard that you want me to do the firebombing and that's it. But I want it all. Put me back on the story and I'll be on top of it."

"Brent's the best reporter in this shop."

Oh, no, he didn't go there. I snapped, "Brent's a North Shore boy. He knows Lincoln Park and the oyster-eaters who live there. This is a South Side story—Englewood and fried shrimp. He doesn't know the community. He doesn't know the people. I doubt if he even knows that Chicago was founded by a black man."

"Don't be patronizing! You blew it!" Bing raged. "Not only did you get beat, Georgia, you didn't answer your page this morning!"

"My pager's broken!" I lied.

"We had to get somebody else on the story, so we sent our top gun."

"C'mon, Bing! This story belongs to me like the last shot belongs to Michael Jordan and you know it."

"It's Brent's ball now."

I picked up the newspaper on his desk. "I don't like being made fun of publicly and I feel responsible for Butter getting on-air. In fact, she wouldn't have gotten on if you hadn't prodded me into it. Remember, Bing?"

God must have struck him deaf and dumb for a minute because he didn't say a mumbling word. Finally, Bing released the pause button on the ten o'clock air-check and turned toward the set. "End of discussion, Georgia."

I had to get back on the story. But how? How could I bump Brent? I went back and sat at my desk and thought about it. Then I got an idea.

I picked up the phone and sat low because I didn't want anyone to interrupt my call. I phoned Butter's house. Kelly answered; I knew her voice by now. "Kelly, hi, it's Georgia."

"Heard anythin'?" she asked.

"No, but I know personally that the police are working very hard on the case—"

"Reverend says—"

"Kelly, I know what Reverend Walker thinks. I saw the paper today. Detective Eckart asked your family not to tell anyone about the gang connection."

"I know, but Reverend told Mama it would be better to shake up things. He said that would help.

Reverend's the one who called the newspaper reporter."

"I respect the Reverend," I said, without adding that I was mad as a bear at him, "but I got nailed in that article and I've been doing nothing but trying to help you from the very beginning."

"I ain't see it. We didn't say nothing bad about you. Mama likes you. Trip too. We just want Butter back. Later for all the rest of that stuff."

"I know. That's all I want, too, Butter back home safe. You believe that don't you, Kelly?"

"Yes, I do."

"Okay. I want to stay on this story, but to do that I need a favor. I need this favor bad so we can keep working together and get Butter back."

"What?"

"TV reporters are going to be calling you up for interviews today."

"Yeah, Channel 3 and 10 called already!"

"Okay, now my station is sending a reporter out named Brent Manning—"

"He called, too, said he'd be by."

"Right. Kelly, don't talk to him. Give the other stations their interviews, but don't talk to Brent. Tell him you don't feel comfortable talking to anyone at my station but me. Period."

"Okay, no one but you at Channel 8."

"Right."

"Okay, I promise and I'll make sure he don't get in. Nobody but you, Georgia."

"Thanks, Kelly. I've got a feeling I'll be seeing you fairly soon."

I hung up, signed on to my computer. I checked the assignment desk's daily log. It listed the stories we were covering, the reporter assigned, and the crew sent with the reporter. The log entry read: Missing Kid. Manning. Unit 23. Great! They'd sent Brent with Zeke because he's been covering the story with me and knows the area and all the players. But Zeke hates Brent Manning as much as I do. I called his truck and prayed that he was in it.

"Unit 23!" Zeke answered.

"Zeke, it's Georgia but don't let on."

"Yeah."

"Is Brent in the truck with you?"

"Yeah, I keep telling you maintenance guys that something smells shitty in here."

"So you know they took me off the story and put him on."

"Yeah."

"I need your help, and I know you can't stand Brent any more than I can."

"Yeah, man, I really want to get this smell out of my truck!"

"Great. Do me a favor. When you get to the Stewart house, they're not going to let you in—"

"Really?"

"—I asked them to freeze out Brent so I can get back on this story—"

"I hear you."

"—but he'll never tell the powers that be back here that he can't get in for an interview. Zeke, I need you to call back to the station, rant and rave that we're not going to have anything, and that we'll get totally beat unless they get me back out there!"

"Okey-dokey! No problem. See ya!"

I faked a call or two, treading water until Zeke's call came in. I wasn't going to set up squat unless it was about Butter.

Within the hour I heard a rumbling up at the assignment desk. I saw a couple of the managers get crazy, concerned looks on their faces. Clarice looked up and across the newsroom at me, smiled, then dropped her eyes back to the computer in front of her. I saw the managers each take a phone. I heard their voices rise. I saw Bing come out of his office and stomp right up to the assignment desk and start a powwow.

I started singing to myself "Respect," by Aretha-know-she-can-sang-Franklin. I only made it through two "sock it to me's" when . . .

"Georgia!" they called out.

I'd gotten my story out of the pit bull's mouth. I wondered what the pit bull, Brent Manning, was going to say?

TWELVE

_____

*T*his is bullshit! Bullshit!" Manning was shouting on the phone inside the news truck. Even with the windows rolled up I could still hear him bellowing and berating and victimizing whoever had the sorry-ass luck of being on the other end of the line.

A courier had driven me out to the location so I could hook up with my crew, and the courier would drive Manning back to the station. A courier's job is to transport for the station: pick up packages, take tapes to a crew, drive reporters to one location or another. Transport. That was the plan. But there was just one little lump in this bowl of grits: Brent Manning didn't want to go. He was still in the live truck. The cartoon section back at the TV station didn't call Brent ahead of time and tell him that they were pulling him off the story. They wanted to avoid his wrath until the last possible moment.

"You pull me now," Brent threatened, "then don't put me back on this story *ever!* I'm not a yo-yo—I'm the best talent in the city of Chicago. I will not be treated otherwise."

Zeke was standing on the driver's side of the truck leaning on the hood laughing his butt off. Brent had locked him out of his own unit because he'd figured out that Zeke had dropped a dime on him back at the station.

I was on the passenger side waiting for Brent to give me the tape he shot during the cop ride-along, which I'd need as an element in my version of today's developments.

Finally Brent Manning hung up the phone and got out of the truck. He walked right past me, got into the courier's car, and slammed the door. Brent was trying to take the tape with him and leave me hanging. *You got the wrong one, baby.* I ran up to the window and banged on the glass as hard as I could. "I need the tape, Brent!"

He said something to the courier and the car started rolling back in reverse.

"Brent! C'mon, gimme the tape!" I shouted and hit the glass again.

By now Zeke was standing on the street on the driver's side and the poor courier just threw up his hands and put the car in park. Brent rolled down the window, tossed the tape out, and rolled the window back up.

"Wheee-doggy!" Zeke laughed as we watched

the courier car speed away. "Testy jack-off, ain't he?"

Channel 3 and Channel 10 had their trucks parked outside. "Bet it's crowded in there," Zeke said, looking over at Butter's house. But I barely heard him. My mind was on screening Brent's tape to see what was on it because I'd have to write around it for my two-minute story. But since it was so hot and would be even hotter sitting inside the truck playing the tape, I got Zeke to fill me in.

"Georgia, it's just standard stuff . . . knocking on doors handing out flyers. The beat cop talked about how dangerous it was on the street, how quiet it had been, and how he knows that something's going to pop soon."

"Great. It's no biggie then." I was confident that I could write to the video cold, so we headed up to the house.

"Hey!" Trip said, answering the door. Butter's cousin peeped around Zeke and me with a hateful expression on his face. "That white man gone?"

"Hey watch it! I'm a white man!"

Trip's eyes narrowed, then he kind of pouted. "You okay though."

Zeke smiled at him, then rubbed the back of his neck. Trip giggled at the sign of affection.

Inside, I recognized two reporters from the other stations. They were good reporters, competitive but fair. One was interviewing Miss Mabel and the other was talking to Kelly.

The living room was crowded with everyone's gear. It's expensive and heavy. The camera costs about thirty grand. The other accessories—tripod, lights, battery belt, case, Beta tapes—another twenty-five grand. Zeke was lugging around about forty pounds worth of stuff and the heat wasn't helping a bit. Zeke wearily added his equipment to the pile because I told him we needed to hang tight. Why piggyback off the comp? Naw, that's stale. I'd wait until they finished and do my own interview. The lights added a heat inside the front room that set me to sweating. I asked Trip, "Can I have a glass of water?"

Trip grabbed me by the hand and started pulling. "C'mon!" He led me back into the kitchen.

"Where's Reverend Walker?" I asked.

"He talked to them other reporters and left when he heard Aunt Kelly talkin' to you. Said he had somewhere else to be."

Uh-huh, he knows he was wrong. Reverend Walker obviously didn't want to face me after the way he bulldozed Doug's plan and got that story in the paper.

"I'll getcha a glass!" Trip said, opening up one of the low cabinets. Inside there were six plates, rose patterned, old and chipped, but sparkling clean. And there were six clear glasses and four yellow plastic tumblers. Trip grabbed two tumblers. "I don't mess wit' them glasses, Grandma crazy 'bout them glasses." He handed the tumblers to me and said, "Bugs. Rinse."

I let the water run and it came out pink.

"Rusty pipes," Trip said. "Keep running it."

I continued to let the faucet run. Soon the water was clear, but I just didn't want to drink it. And I didn't want to embarrass Trip.

I said, "Hey, how 'bout instead of just plain old water to cool us off, why don't we get some ice cream?"

"Yeah!" Trip's eyes got wide and a grin opened up from one side of his face to the other. "Eskimo bars!"

"Let's go, my man."

August in Chicago is nothing to play with. Outside, the blistering white rays were putting a real hurting on everything they touched. Trip and I stood on the shady porch for a couple of minutes trying to get up our courage to venture out farther.

Next door a battle of checkers was going on. Both men were sitting on plastic milk crates, their skin a deep chocolate brown. Both were bald, one by nature, the other by razor. The older man had a neat, ice white beard and he wore blunt-legged khaki shorts and a sleeveless cotton undershirt. As he studied the board, he squeezed the ends of a white terry-cloth towel that was roped around his neck.

His young rival had on long-legged shorts four sizes too big belted as low as they could go on his hips to show off the waistband of his white Calvin Klein briefs. He was shirtless and looked too cool given how hot it was.

Trip spoke to the young brother. "You beatin', T-Bob?"

T-Bob smiled and touched his chin.

"Don't you got something to do, Trip?" the elderly man barked. "G'on to it."

Trip grinned at me and said, "Let's go!"

Two steps outside of the front gate and both of

us were using the back of our hands to wipe away the
sweat from our faces. We were only walking three
blocks to a corner store but the heat bench-pressing
against our bodies slowed us down considerably.

People in the neighborhood watched us walk
down the street. The few people sitting outside were
stretched out beneath double awnings or large trees.

"Butter. . . ." Trip pointed at a Xeroxed flyer with
his cousin's picture on it. Handwritten below the picture were the words: MISSING GIRL and a brief
description of Butter. The flyer was taped to a light
pole. Everyone was helping to look for Butter.

"The folks around here must really love Butter."

"Yep," Trip responded, then waved at a group of
little boys around his age.

They shouted, "Where y'all goin', Trip?"

"Sto'!"

"Cobs!" one of the boys yelled, the South Side
slang for "gimme some." "Man, cobs on whatever it
is you get!"

"You got enough money for 'em? They're my
friends."

"Sure," I said and placed my hand on Trip's
shoulder. He shook it off and looked up at me. "Sissy
stuff."

I got the sense that Trip was trying very hard to
be a man before his time. "You like living here, Trip?
I mean, are you scared sometimes with all the shooting and stuff that goes on?"

"Scared! I ain't scared of nothing and nobody.
Ain't no sissy walking with you."

"Trip, it's not sissy to be afraid. Sometimes it's

120

smart. Fear can tell you when to stay away from something. Fear can keep you safe sometimes. If you're afraid of something or somebody, it's best to get away from it as fast as you can."

"Sounds sissy to me. I've gotta watch out for my mama, grandma, auntie, and Butter."

"That's good, and you have to study hard in school, that's a way of helping, too, making sure you go to college and . . ."

Trip shrugged, then started throwing punches in the air. "I'ma be a boxer like Holyfield or some of them. I can beat anybody 'round here my size or a little bigger."

"You still need to hit those books," I said, and playfully grabbed Trip around the neck. He smiled.

"Say, you know Oprah?" Trip asked. "I wanna have dinner with Oprah—but real food, not that diet stuff she always talkin' 'bout."

"No, I don't know Oprah." Everybody in Chicago thinks everybody else in TV knows Oprah. "But I can get you tickets to see one of her shows, how about that? When this is all over, how 'bout that, huh? Me, you, Butter . . . all of us will go, huh?"

That cheered Trip up, and we finally made it to the store. Thank you, Jesus! Trip opened the big white freezer nestled against the tan metal counter and a gush of arctic air made us both moan with exhausted relief.

"I could climb in there now and just go to sleep," I said.

"Me, too," Trip agreed. He grabbed a box of Eskimo bars. "Six in here. Umh, there's Grandma,

Auntie Kelly, Zeke, you, and two for me! Get another box for my friends, that's theirs, okay?"

"Done."

We left the store, each carrying a box, but just as we cleared the doorway, Trip stopped suddenly. The boy didn't move and his face drained of color as he clutched the box of Eskimo bars.

"Trip? What is it?"

Then I knelt down and followed his line of vision across the street to an abandoned building. And there I saw what he saw and a question popped into my head as I tried to calm down Trip. Where had I seen that T-shirt before?

THIRTEEN

I saw two people in the doorway. One of them wore a black T-shirt with white letters that said BE something. Where had I seen that shirt before?

Trip was running toward the doorway, staring straight ahead, not even blinking, clutching the box of Eskimo bars he was holding.

I reached for him and missed. "Trip!"

The two people, a man and a woman, were huddled together, hunched over in the doorway. The wooden beams obstructed their faces by creating a black fan of shade. The woman leaned back to reveal the full lettering on the back of the shirt: BE NO. 1 it read.

I reached the doorway a few steps behind Trip, panting as the heat billowed steam from my lungs and sweat dropped down my chin. Then the woman turned and looked out, the sunlight catching her face. It was Trip's mother, Angel, wearing the T-shirt Butter had won at the spelling contest. She was sitting cross-legged with her head bobbing slowly. Angel was high as a telephone pole.

The man with her had on a torn button-down shirt with a long piece hanging down in the back that was shaped like the closing flap of an envelope. His hipbones jutted out just half a palm's length beneath the tiny spiral bands of his rib cage. A salty crust of mucus rimmed his nostrils as he periodically looked up and down. He was high, too, but apparently not as waxed as Angel.

"Why you gotta be wearin' Butter's favorite shirt, doin' your dirty business?" Trip yelled at his mother.

Startled, Angel's hands shook and she looked up at Trip and moaned groggily. "G'on Trip!"

The man turned toward Trip and said firmly, "Don't talk to your mother like that."

That's when I saw the eyes that I knew, the ones that had made me giggle with my girlfriends at the pep rally over how cute he was. . . . The ones that had looked understanding but disappointed when I refused to cut class and go home with him for my first sexual experience.

"A.J.?" I asked. He looked so bad, my heart ached for him. A.J. used to be *fine* and the smartest boy on the block. "A.J., it's Georgia."

"Hey, girl," he summoned up after he looked at me for a long time without blinking. "How'd you get out of the TV set?"

I winced. "A.J., what-what . . ."

"I'm cool. I'm just hanging out here with Angel. Everything is cool."

Trip was now begging his mother, "Let's go home, Mama! Let's go home!"

Angel was shaking her head no. A.J. spoke to me: "Georgia, I see you. You've done good. Mama watches you all the time."

"Thanks, A.J. What can I do to help you, huh?"

"Mama, get up and let's go, Mama!"

"Give me some money," A.J. said. "I don't have nothing."

"I can't give you any money, A.J., but here, take my card and if you want to get some help for this drug thing, call me. You're better than this, A.J."

A.J. took the card reluctantly. *Good, there's hope.* Then he began picking his teeth with it. I dropped my eyes.

At first Angel only seemed to see Trip, and then her gaze included me, and her face melted into this mass of hatred. Trip backed away and stood directly in front of me. I felt his back against my stomach. The box of Eskimo bars I held cracked, and I could feel their coolness through the paper box.

"Don't you look at me!" Angel yelled at me.

But how could I not look? Her face was ugly with the scorn it was showing, uglier than any of the keloid tissue covering her drug-scarred arms.

How could I not look? She had Trip's eyes. And was wearing Butter's favorite shirt, which she had won at the spelling contest.

How could I not look? Even though I'd done stories, been on the street and knew I was no novice, the emotion and fear, anger and helplessness of this woman was more real and more personal to me than anything I'd ever reported.

A.J. touched Angel's arm. "Quiet, baby. Quiet down." But she yelled at me again, "Don't look at me!"

The gooey, sticky wetness of the melting ice cream pressed against my hands. I started pulling Trip away, backing out of the doorway.

"That's right, take my baby on home."

I pulled him away and forced him to walk down the street. "Forget it. Let's just go, Trip."

Trip mumbled as we walked away, "Messin' up Butter's stuff."

And that's all he said as we walked back to the house. Our silence was as dense as the heat around us. I looked back twice at A.J. This man was wasted, his life off course.

I looked down at Trip and wondered about what he could be. I didn't want the same ugly thing to happen to him. I wanted to help Trip but I knew he wouldn't accept that from me. I didn't know him well enough right now to really reach him.

"Hey, man, cobs!" the group of boys shouted at us as we neared the house. "We already said it, cobs!"

Trip played them off cold-bloodedly. He just kept walking.

I handed the boys the box of Eskimo bars I was carrying. They tore it open and one of the boys yelled, "They busted!"

"Shut up before I bust your head!" Trip yelled over his shoulder as he went through the gate and back into the house.

I stayed a few steps behind, trying to give Trip his mental and physical space.

Zeke was all set up for the interview, his lights in place. "What's wrong with Mighty Mouse?" Zeke asked as Trip blew right past him.

"Nothing, just the heat," I said. I wasn't going to tell Trip's business. If Trip wanted outsiders to know, let him tell them. Miss Mabel and Kelly looked at me; they knew. I didn't have to say. Neither did Trip.

"Well." Zeke shrugged. "I'm about ready to do this interview. Let's go. Say, you didn't bring your cameraman any ice cream?" Zeke turned around and yelled toward the kitchen where Trip had disappeared. "Hey, kid, how about sharing some of that ice cream?"

Zeke checked his lights again and when Trip didn't bring the ice cream he asked me, "Get me a bar, would you, Georgia?"

Zeke liked to be catered to and because he was such a good shooter nearly all the reporters obliged him. I went into the kitchen and Trip . . . was gone. I opened the back door and looked out. He was nowhere to be seen.

The box of Eskimo bars was on the counter. I grabbed the box, went out to the front room, and gave Zeke one; Miss Mabel and Kelly said no thank you. I did the interview, asking the two women how they felt now that Butter had been missing for three days. I asked about their hopes and their dreams. I wanted the audience not only to know Butter but to get a feel for her family as well. We set up a signal in the truck, beamed back my interview plus the video

127

and the cop interview from the ride-along that Manning had done.

I'd have everything that everyone else had except maybe a neighbor sound bite, a quick quote. No big deal. And you know what? I decided to bag it all. Just forget it. *Next.* I called the producer and told him that I wanted him to do the firebombing story as a long voice-over to a sound bite from the police before tossing to me live. That would be the transition for me to do a live interview with Miss Mabel and Kelly from inside Butter's own room.

I didn't want to go live from outside the house as I knew everyone else was doing. Even though Channel 8's primary audience is 180 degrees different from Butter's family—mostly older white viewers with money—I wanted to let them know that Butter could be *their* missing child. I wanted them to know that a poor African-American grandmother and mother hurt and worry over a missing child just as much as well-to-do parents like the college professor and his wife.

This story wasn't just about gangs in the ghetto snatching an eyewitness. To Channel 8's core audience, that's something that happens to *those people.* But a grandmother worrying about her little girl? A mother looking for a child whom she can't find? Those things hit home with everyone.

That's what television news should be. But TV news is getting away from the guts of a story, the people, the human side of a story. That's ground zero. And that's where I decided to be. I was going there.

Zeke bitched awhile about laying all that cable from the truck into the house. But he figured a way to go through the window to shorten the distance. I called over the little boys I had given the ice cream to, gave them three dollars apiece and told them not to let anyone go near the truck while I was on-air.

Zeke took the camera off the tripod that holds it steady during a sit-down interview. I told him to shoulder it and just go with us. I had him put clip mikes on Miss Mabel's and Kelly's collars so they could move around with me.

The director back at the station told me that my hit time, the exact time I was to air during the five o'clock show was five-0-one-ten. One minute and ten seconds after five. I told Kelly and Miss Mabel not to be nervous and to talk about Butter and move around the kids' room. I told them to be natural, to just talk to me as they had been doing all day. I prayed that this would work.

"I'm here live with Mabel and Kelly Stewart. They are Butter's grandmother and mother. You've met them before. We've brought you continuous coverage of the search for Butter, who has been missing now for three days. Miss Mabel, tell us, what kind of a child is Butter?"

Zeke pushed into a shot of Miss Mabel; her hands were shaking as she sat on Butter's bed, clutching the girl's pink pillow with unicorns all over it. "My Butter likes these animals, sitting here. She's a smart chile, sit here and read books all the time and don't bother anyone, just curl up wit' a book and her animals. . . ."

There were about a dozen stuffed animals, bears, tigers, a hippo against the wall. Zeke panned them with the camera, then pulled back to Miss Mabel.

". . . Trip won most of these at one of them street carnivals they begged to go tah. I ain't have the money. But I found some extra that day . . . umm-huh . . . and give the money to the kids so they could go. Butter hugged my neck and said, 'Thank you, Gran, you the best gran in the world.' My Butter said that to me."

Miss Mabel brought her index finger, curled and shaking, to her lips, as if she had a secret to keep to herself. Miss Mabel was clearly trying to hold her emotions in check and it worked for just about five seconds. But all that sadness and fear whipping around inside of her wouldn't stay put, forcing a tear to go public, freely displaying her pain.

Zeke panned over to Kelly, who was sitting at a little plastic drawing table like a lot of little children have. There were sketches Butter had made on pieces of paper. A house. A horse. A car. Kids on a playground. Kelly looked at Butter's work, her eyes coming alive. She seemed to be gathering together pieces of happy times, hugging them like a child hugs a favorite toy.

"These Butter's pictures," Kelly said softly. "She likes to draw and color. Go broke tryin' ta keep the girl in Crayolas and books. This her favorite, this house here with the blue top and white bottom. She says, 'Mama, I wanna live in a pretty house like this one day.' That's why I work nights and take my business classes during the day at Kennedy-King College, so I can get my degree and do better for all us. Now I don't care 'bout nothing, I just want my baby Butter back home . . ."

Zeke pulled out his shot to include me. I ended the live shot by updating the story: "There have been no signs of Butter. Several reputed members of the Rockies have been brought in for questioning, and the neighborhood has been quiet. The gangs, police say, are hiding underground and tensions are mounting. Georgia Barnett, Channel 8 News, back to you in the newsroom."

When I ended my live shot, Zeke popped his head out away from the camera lens and winked at me. I smiled just as one of the kids stationed outside by the live truck yelled, "Your car phone is ringing!" I went outside and answered it.

"Georgia, fuckin' fabulous! Fuckin' fabulous! That was great. You're a goddess!" It was Bing, gushing kudos and heaping praise. I was pleased, but in television news I know you're a hero one minute and a butt head the next. It changed from story to story, from deadline to deadline.

Zeke came out to the truck. I gave him a thumbs-up and he grinned. In the middle of all this my pager went off. It was Doug. I cut Bing off, telling him I had to catch an interview. I hung up and dialed Doug.

"Got a tip for you," he said.

Finally! I'd been playing by his rules for the longest and now Doug was giving me a play. "What's going on?"

He began talking about the drive-by shooting case. "That last victim in the hospital? The one in critical?"

"Yeah, the teenage girl."

"Right. She just died. The Rockies and the Bandits have been cool about this feud 'cause we've put so much heat on them. That's why nothing has jumped off so far. They've got Butter and now she's more than a witness to a drive-by; now it's murder."

I pictured Little Cap and remembered his lengthy criminal record. I mumbled, "With Little Cap's rap sheet, he'll land on death row. And I don't mean records. I mean Stateville Prison."

"Bad joke."

"Sorry, I'm nervous and sometimes a bad joke will calm me down."

"Georgia, my bones tell me something's going to give and give real soon."

"What does that mean for Butter?" I said, fear rushing up inside of me.

Silence.

"Doug, talk to me."

"Georgia, what do you want me to say?"

"I want you to say that you guys are going to find her. The Chicago PD can't find a little girl? Now I'm getting like Reverend Walker. Are you guys trying hard enough?"

"The last thing I need is you jumping in my stuff. I've got that bad press from Reverend Walker and the chief of detectives is on my back demanding daily updates. Don't give me grief. You should be glad I called you up to help you out."

Doug's salty response made me angry. "One little tip you gave me," I said. "I've been playing your game the entire time, Doug."

"All you've got to deal with is getting your story on the air, Georgia. That's no big deal! I'm a detective and I'm dealing with some heavy shit here."

"And I'm not? I'm sent out here every day to look at their faces—Miss Mabel and Kelly, and Trip's, too. I have to look at Butter's stuffed animals and her bed that hasn't been slept in and I'm worryin' about this child like she's mine. Hear me, Doug?"

Of course he didn't. He had hung up on me.

Zeke came walking out of the house. Extra lengths of cable were looped around his neck, arms, and waist as if he'd gotten caught by some black-tailed reptile from Jurassic Park. "What's next, Georgia?" he asked.

"Community Hospital."

FOURTEEN

Zeke should have been an ambulance driver. One, because we passed an ambulance, beating it to the hospital. And two, because I always seem to need a stretcher after riding in the truck with him. But I can't complain too much because Zeke got me there in plenty of time to snoop out my story.

We pulled into a no parking zone right in front of the hospital. I eased out of the truck, shaking as usual from Zeke's psycho driving and unsettled as all get-out because of this latest turn of events.

I may have been unsettled but I didn't forget how to do my job, how to cover my story. I had called ahead to the hospital media director, who was not available. I called the nurses' station and got a supervisor who wouldn't comment and referred me to the media director. I called another source at the cop shop, but my source said to call the hospital. The entire scenario put me in mind of Billy Preston's song "Will It Go Round in Circles."

I wanted to reconfirm my tip from Doug that the girl was dead. Not that I didn't believe him, it was just a habit of mine to double-check everything if I could. I needed background on this new angle of the story. I was not about to get caught with my panties down.

On the day of the drive-by I had the lead story at the scene and another reporter was live at the hospital doing a sidebar story on the five shooting victims. I called back to the station and asked Clarice to go pull the sidebar package from that day. She found the tape, took it into a screening room where she played it, and held the phone up to the speaker so I could hear and take notes.

Reporter Ada Gonzales's voice sounded rusty coming through over the car phone line:

"And the most critical victim is seventeen-year-old Jackie Martin. She was sitting on her front steps when two bullets hit her in the chest and hip. Doctor Adam Chu says that Martin lost a great deal of blood and that her wounds are life-threatening."

Then I heard a sound bite from the doctor, who said the next twenty-four hours would be critical for the patient; he noted her youth and said that the bullet was lodged deep in the chest cavity. A few more inches and there wouldn't be any need for a press conference, he concluded.

Gonzales's reporter track continued:

"In an ironic twist, two of Martin's relatives retired from this facility—one as a lab assistant and the other as a janitor. The Martin family is holding vigil here twenty-four hours a day. Family members divide their time between Jackie's room and this table inside the hospital's cafeteria. It's a base, if you will, where relatives wait their turn to visit with Jackie. They say some family member will keep up the vigil here until the seventeen-year-old girl is out of danger. . . ."

Now I knew right where to go. Zeke and I headed into the hospital cafeteria and went straight to the table of worried-looking people. There sitting huddled together was the family of Jackie Martin. As I approached the table, I told Zeke to roll but point his camera to the floor first. I held the mike at my side and said, "Excuse me. My name is Georgia Barnett, with Channel 8 news. I'm very sorry about the death of Jackie. I know that this is a tough time for the family but we'd"—then I nodded to Zeke who raised his camera—"like to talk to you about this tragedy."

"Excuse me!" A hand grabbed my mike. It was the hospital security guard. "Did you get clearance to be inside here?"

"Of course," I lied instantly.

"I don't see any passes!"

I picked up one that was on the edge of the table. "See?"

The security guard knew something wasn't right and he looked confused.

"Go, Georgia, we've got a deadline," Zeke said, stepping in front of the guard, who backed off and left.

I had to burn rubber now. The guard was going to go check my story. I had to get as much as I could before he came back to toss us out on our tails. I turned to a slim young brother in his early twenties with large sleepy eyes, caramel-colored skin, and wispy, high-arching eyebrows. He was sitting in the booth, his arm limp behind the split vinyl of the seat. He turned to me and said, "I'm Jackie's brother, Jason."

"With Jackie's death," I asked gently, "what do you want people to know about your sister?"

"Jackie was going to be somebody. She went to school and got good grades and was in no trouble whatsoever. She was just in the wrong place at the wrong time."

"With the wrong person you mean!" This from a woman who was sitting at the head of the table, her shoulders slumped down, slim hands resting on her forearms. Dark lines creased her cheeks and her skin was the shiny, baked brown of pie crust. She had the solemn demeanor that was expected of a senior citizen placed in a dire situation such as this. "Jackie hung out with that no-good Negro entirely too much!"

"Ssssh, Auntie Vee—" someone whispered.

"Ssssh, nothin', if she hadn't been sittin' there with that no-good T-Bob—you better believe they was shootin' at him. I'm tired! Hear? Tired. Now Jackie is gone. And Lord knows what's happened to little Butter."

"Don't air that part about T-Bob," Jason said in a low yet stern voice. "We don't want any trouble."

"Do you live in the same neighborhood?"

"They do. I got sent to live in Connecticut with some cousins eight years ago when the gangs tried to jump me in. I've been living there ever since. I have my two-year degree and I'm working for a real estate broker. The first thing I want to do after the funeral is look for a house and move my family out of Chicago, away from the old neighborhood."

I got a couple of more sound bites from Jason. No other family member wanted to talk. I asked him, off the record, about T-Bob.

"T-Bob was nothing but a little shorty when I left." Jason laughed. When his voice stopped I could hear the crinkle of stubble as he rubbed an emerging beard. For a young man, he was looking very old right now. "T-Bob hung out with Jackie and her best friend, Karen, all the time," Jason went on. "I know he was trying to get some play from one of them, but I couldn't figure out which one. Now my family is down on T-Bob because he hasn't come 'round since Jackie got shot. He was sitting in the middle of the girls when the drive-by happened. I heard T-Bob grabbed them around the neck and tried to roll out of the way, but Jackie was on the outside and got caught."

"You say your family is hard on him. Obviously you don't feel the same way?"

"I know it's rough out there . . . I know the streets are bad . . . but T-Bob, yeah, he could have come to visit her. But it's tough. I'm not saying it's his fault because I was on the streets once and I know how the pressure can get to you. But T-Bob could have called the house or something, you know?"

"You're sure he's gangbanging?"

"In that neighborhood? What teenager isn't?"

"Hey!" The security guard was back. "Let's go!"

I gave Zeke my "Think he's mad?" look as we started to make a quick exit. "Jason, do you have a picture of Jackie?" I managed to ask.

"Umm, no. But my auntie might."

The guard was pushing us out. "Hey! Hey!" Zeke yelled. "Get your hands off my fanny!"

A few of the cafeteria workers started laughing, while I shouted over my shoulder, "Bring it outside, please?"

Jason waved okay.

We went outside to kill time before our ten o'clock live shot, when we ran into Reverend Walker. "Georgia Barnett! You're everywhere," he said politely.

"And so are you," I answered back just as politely. "You know the Martin family?" I asked, and out of the corner of my eye I glimpsed Zeke already on the case changing videotapes so he could start rolling as soon as possible.

"Of course. The Martin family attends services at my church. I also have a door-to-door ministry. I'm familiar with all the families in the neighborhood."

Reverend Walker saw Zeke aiming the camera at him and he cleared his throat and straightened his tie. "I'm going inside," he said, looking right into the camera, "to console the family. I was here earlier in the day."

"Don't look at the camera, look at me, Reverend," I instructed him. "Tell me what this latest tragedy means to the community."

"It's yet another sign of the devastation in inner-city communities spurred on by joblessness, hopelessness, and ungodliness. The economy is in a shambles and young men in these gangs have no jobs, and no prospects. They are idle and they are angry. They turn to easy money by peddling drugs and easy fun, which to them is violence."

"So you're saying if there were more jobs in the community there would be fewer gangs and gang violence?"

"Yes, more jobs and more teachers and more programs. Our young people need guidance. And we need more police presence. Since I got the *Defender* to do Butter's story, media coverage has increased and it's put pressure on the police to do their jobs. I've seen more police patrols in the last few days than I've seen for months on end prior to this. It's too late for Jackie Martin. . . . We hope it's not too late for Butter Johnson."

"Do you want to say anything to the people who have Butter?"

"Yes. Turn her loose. That child is a baby and wouldn't harm a fly. Harm her and the wrath of God shall rain down like fire."

The Right Reverend was over the top. He played heavy to Zeke's camera.

"But I'm not just talking about something needing to be done," Reverend Walker preached. "I'm going to do something. Tomorrow evening I'm going to lead a march through the park."

"What's the march called?" Doesn't every march have its own name nowadays?

"It will be called the Healing and the Hope Vigil. Healing for the wounds left by the untimely death of young Jackie. And hope for the safe return of Butter. We'll march through the neighborhood, five blocks to the park. Anyone who wants to bring about a change is welcome to join. Eight P.M. I hope to see you there?"

"Channel 8 News will be there," I said to Reverend Walker. I told Zeke, "Cutaways." He began circling to shoot various wide shots of us standing and talking. With cutaway video you can show a wide shot, then go to a tight shot, and it looks like a natural change, as opposed to video shifting or jumping all over the place. You have to stand in your same position. While Zeke shot cutaways, Reverend Walker and I exchanged hopes for Butter's safe return.

"I got enough," Zeke said with a hard sniff as he snapped off the overhead light on his camera.

"I hope to see you at the rally," Reverend Walker said. Then he paused and mumbled sheepishly, "I heard from Butter's family that you were angry about the *Defender* article."

"That's old and over with. I know you did what you thought best for Butter and her family." I thought, And for yourself.

"God bless," Reverend Walker said, touching the cross at his neck. He turned and walked through the automatic doors of the hospital.

I started scribbling notes on my pad. I was about halfway finished writing my story when out of the corner of my eye I saw Doug standing there. The hazy yellow light above the emergency entrance hit him just right as he stepped out of the shadows. He had on a dark blue T-shirt, tight-fitting jeans, and a big brass belt buckle in the shape of a clenched fist.

"Georgia?" he called.

I looked back down at my notes, up at the sky, down the street—any way but his way. I was still a little bit mad at Doug for hanging up on me earlier in the evening.

Zeke was sitting on the edge of the open door of the truck. "Hey, Georgia, Detective Midnight is callin' you."

I just looked at Zeke and rolled my eyes. Didn't he ever know when to shut up?

"C'mon, Georgia, I want to talk to you."

"She's gotta go live in ten minutes," Zeke said to Doug.

Just did not know when to shut up. *Ever.*

At that moment Jason came down with the picture. It was a color photo of Jackie at her junior prom. She had her hair swept up in the back, two long twisted strands down by her ears, and tiny pale blue flowers around a beautiful headband. "Nice," I breathed admiringly.

Zeke came over and I held the picture for him. He zoomed in and focused. We would beam back video of the picture to the station where the graphics department would use computer software to cut out Jackie's image alone, soften the edges, increase the clarity, and mount the picture on a blue background with her name printed at the bottom.

The entire time Doug stood up against the side wall, his hands stuffed in his pockets. He watched us work. I prepared to go live, practicing what I would say. Zeke was setting up the shot.

When I got a break, Doug came over and spoke firmly. "Georgia, I came down here to say I'm sorry. When you finish, come over to my car. I'll be there waiting."

Zeke popped his head out from behind the camera. "I know you ain't going for that."

"Will you shut up, Zeke?"

"That's what my wife says to me all the time, Shut up, Zeke. That's all I get out of a woman is shut up . . . no hugs, no kisses, no pus—"

"Zeke!"

He stooped down and started fiddling with the cable, mumbling, "Women . . ."

I got through the live shot, which included my piece that had the produced picture of Jackie, file footage of the drive-by scene, exterior of the hospital, sound bites from the family and from Reverend Walker. When I finished the car was still there, parked by a fire hydrant—isn't that just like a cop?

I walked up to the passenger-side window, which Doug had rolled all the way down. He had his seat back, and his arms crossed over his broad chest. His tired eyes slowly turned toward me.

"Say, mister," I said, "I'm just getting off work. I don't feel like waiting for a cab. Can you give a sister a lift?"

"Sure." Doug smiled. "Where to?"

FIFTEEN

*Y*ou ah dirty dog, but I got ah hold of your leash . . ."
As Doug and I got out of the car, I could hear my
twin cutting up with one of the blues songs she'd
written. Doug and I hadn't said much in the car, a
simple exchange of sorrys. I suggested we unwind at
my sister Peaches's place.

"Awwwwww, baby . . ." Peaches wailed.

We got to the door, and as usual, Milton was sitting there just bobbing his head and popping his fingers. He looked up at us, winked at me, and asked
Doug for ten dollars.

Doug looked at me. Please . . . *free?* Peaches
owes me too much money for that. "Pay the man,
Doug."

" *. . . You ah dirt-ay, dirt-ay doe-whog . . .*"

Milton took the ten-dollar bill and warmly welcomed us with his traditional, "Go on in, and good times."

"*. . . but I gotta fist full of your leash . . . !*"

Peaches was at that point in the song where she was hunched all the way down to the floor. I stopped Doug and warned him, "You have to step back for this part." I eased us off to the side of the stage. Peaches was about to do what I called her nasty dance.

Peaches started singing, ". . . I'm tuggin', rubbin', kissin', and huggin' . . ."

She worked her way down to a squat and then started doing a twist coming back up but slow, like a good old-fashioned up-against-the-wall grind. She worked the word "huggin'" over and over again.

The piano man was hitting four notes at the same time, in two different octaves. Dude was sweating and pounding the keys until they sounded like they were shrieking. Peaches was contorting and straddling the mike stand. The infamous nasty dance. The first time my grandmother caught her doing it, she chased Peaches down a dirt road with a switch.

When we were teenagers, Peaches used to practice this with a broom and call it her witch twist. Tonight when she got all the way up on her toes, she kicked off one of her pumps. Actually, it was one of my pumps. Every time the chick came over to my place to visit, she raided my shoe closet. The red satin scud went sailing through the air. Ten sets of men's hands went rebounding after that shoe. I reminded myself to put a Master lock on my shoe closet door.

"Wow!" Peaches laughed into the mike and started walking the stage peg-legged, singing and shouting.

A regular, the proud owner of a countrified Gomer Pyle voice, shouted, "Peaches! Peaches! Peaches!"

"Man!" Doug said, his face brilliant with pleasure, which made him even more handsome. "Your sister is something!"

"Yep!" I said very proudly.

Rita the hostess came over to us. That poor chile was forever working her wrist bangles and sipping her drink. Rita tried to seat us at the house table but grudgingly agreed when I asked for a rear booth, out of the range of Hurricane Peaches.

Doug had a shot and beer. I had wine.

"Ahh, yeah," I moaned, not realizing how much I needed a sip-sip of a little something-something.

Doug had the heel of his shot glass up against his forehead, rolling it back and forth. "It's been a crazy few days, huh?"

"Yes, Lord." I sighed and eased down into the lap of the booth. "I called the hospital and they said Audrey Darrington was released. I'm afraid for her—"

"Don't worry. I've got a car stationed outside her house as we speak. But tomorrow her sister is going to drive her to Memphis for a while, till this thing blows over."

"Good, I like Audrey. She's a nice lady."

"With a fucked-up son."

We clicked our drinks, said cheers, and sipped.

I wanted to put all that had happened aside, but

first I had to ask Doug about Jackie's death. What did Jackie's death mean for Butter?

Doug didn't say a word.

What about the trace on the phone call to my house, the one asking for ransom?

Still working, Doug said.

I asked about the prints from the scene beneath the el. Not back yet, Doug said.

Would they kill her? Could she be dead already? Maybe the police should ease up, give the Rockies and the Bandits room and in that space, maybe they would make a mistake.

"Georgia, let's talk about something else, huh? Put the reporter in you aside and I'll put the detective in me aside and let's try something new."

"Like?" I said, flipping the word up into the air.

Doug cocked his head to the left and let the syllable's sound float down between us. When it landed, he said, "Like us."

I felt a little anxious but I played it cool, sipped my drink, and let Doug proceed.

"So . . . Are you married, single, or divorced?"

I'm hanging by a sculptured nail off Mount Late Thirties. I work like a fiend, so meeting a man is tough. But I didn't want to seem too anxious. I simply said, "I'm single."

Doug nodded. Tracing his finger along the rim of the shot glass, he countered, "I'm divorced. It's been about a year and a half."

Okay, enough time to avoid a lot of rebound baggage. And I knew better than to ask what went wrong. I dug in further. "Steady girlfriend?"

"No . . . I have dates but no one special at this point." He spoke clearly, the words anchored by a steady gaze.

Yeah! Doug was already looking good to me; now he was looking *real* good.

"You have any kids?"

"No, no children. . . . I love kids and I wanna have some eventually, but we never got along well enough—or long enough—to plan a family. There's nothing between us now but Lake Michigan and two states."

Could the man look any better to me at all? I don't think so!

"What about you, Georgia, you seeing anyone special?"

"Doug, the only special somebody in my life is my three-year-old nephew, Satch, Peaches's son."

Doug grinned, "Peaches doesn't look like the mothering kind."

"She's actually very good with Satch, better than his father, Mario. He's a drummer—travels all the time and has barely laid eyes on Satch. Mama constantly warned Peaches about him. I did too. She can't say she burned up because nobody yelled fire! We told her."

Doug laughed and the sound tapered to a hush when he gently bit his bottom lip, then smiled. "Your mother should have left Peaches alone. Sounds like she might have inadvertently pushed her into it."

"There's a history there, you see. Mama hated performing—as a young woman she had toured as a singer but she only went into it because my grandmother was an entertainer in Memphis and pushed her into it. But when Mama's career failed and her marriage to my dad did, too, she fled to Chicago. When we were growing up, Mama worked all kinds of jobs and went to night college, too. Then she went to law school part time. The old girl pulled it off— she's a lawyer for the city now."

"Tough lady."

"You said it. And Mama's really tough on Peaches because she didn't want us performing—she wanted us to go to college and have careers. So she and Peaches do a pull and yank thing with each other."

"So when your mother tried to pull Peaches away from this drummer guy, she yanked him in closer."

"Yep, and it blew up in her face. Besides my nephew, the relationship was sour. Peaches has been trying to chase Mario down for child support with no luck."

"That wouldn't happen to you."

"What wouldn't?"

"Having to chase a man down." Doug's voice dropped to a flirtatious whisper but his eyes held mine steadily. "Any guy would be a fool to run away from a beautiful woman like you, no matter what the circumstances."

Hey now! I told myself not to break out into a grin like a Cheshire cat. Don't do it. Don't act like a schoolgirl with raging hormones. But you know I did, grinning like an idiot, and it felt good.

"Georgia . . ." Doug murmured, touching my hand.

"Hey!" Peaches shouted. "What y'all doing back here?" My sister put her hands on her hips and stood wide-legged.

Big-mouth Peaches! Her timing is worse than a busted watch. Does she always have to be the center of attention?

"Peaches, we're trying to have a quiet drink," I finally answered after giving her a hug.

"Quiet?!" She looked from me to Doug and nodded her head. "Georgia ought to know she can't sneak nowhere around me. We got that twin vibe going. We feel what each other feels. I'm Peaches Barnett, and you are?"

"Doug Eckart," he said and shook her hand.

"Don't shake it, kiss it! Demanding ain't I?"

"Always have been . . ." I started to say.

". . . And always will be," Peaches finished my sentence. "How'd y'all hook up?"

"Doug, you'll have to excuse Peaches, she's nosy."

Peaches nudged me with her hips. "Yeah, I'm nosy. Scootch over."

What could I say? I had stuck my straw in her business and sipped many a day. So I gave her a brief synopsis of our working relationship.

"Oh, so you two are working together to try and find that little girl who's missing," Peaches said. "I've been watching you, Georgia. You've been doing a good job with the coverage."

"Excellent," Doug corrected and raised his drink.

"I see." Peaches gave me the eye, and gave me an elbow under the table.

"Then you should be moving on," I said.

Doug chuckled.

"Fine by me," Peaches replied. "Like I said, twins got that feeling vibe going." Peaches got up from the table and slapped Doug on the arm. "Be good now. *When she comes, I come!*"

Call Forever Rest Funeral Home, I could have died I was so embarrassed. Doug, however, was laughing so hard he was up under the table practically, rolling from side to side. I gave Peaches the finger and she blew me a kiss as she sashayed away.

"Doug, let's go. Peaches is not going to let us have a minute's peace, I can see that right now."

"All right. Whatcha feel like?"

"My place."

I blinked hard after I heard my own voice, but that sexy invitation rolled off my tongue with the greatest of ease. I wanted to get to know Doug better. I wanted to relax but I didn't want to be alone. I knew he could understand the tripped-out stress that I was under because he was under it, too. Similar levels of tension can make pals or passion partners out of work associates.

When we entered my apartment I directed Doug to the refrigerator for a cold beer while I cleared off the last picture of Max and me from the coffee table. We nestled down on the sofa and Doug stroked the soft hair at the base of my neck with the back of his hand. I closed my eyes and digested the tingly sensation the touch gave me. We sat very close on my oversized couch, the coolness of the central air pampering our tired bodies. We faced the picture window, Lake Michigan front and center, on a night when tiny stars were splattered across the sky.

Doug's arm around my shoulders held me loosely yet firmly. We had yet to kiss, but this time together seemed very intimate and it reinforced in my mind what I've always been unable to express to most men—that intimacy is very much mental and emotional. How we got in this position, I forget; but it was a satisfying place to be.

Doug happened to like Frankie Beverly and Maze. The sex-me-up voice of Frankie Beverly was ringing in our ears. Our conversation was now nonexistent; we simply relaxed and listened to the music. I began to think about nothing but feeling as good as I possibly could at that moment. No drive-bys, gangbangers, Butter, or anything else. Yes, I needed me some of this!

Finally Doug leaned closer and began to kiss me behind my ear. His breath was like the lush sound of an ocean seashell and I smelled the heady aroma of his masculine body. When I turned my face up, his eyes glittered in the semi-dark room. And then I marveled at the exquisite taste of his lips as they pressed against mine, parting to allow our tongues to greet each other for the first time. A kiss is more than a kiss when you lose all sense of time.

We embraced each other, snuggling close on the couch. I was so relaxed, more than I'd been in days. I dropped my tired head back and melted. Doug's breathing became smoother and smoother. "You feel good," he whispered. "Close your eyes and let go."

We seemed weightless together and the music became softer.

That's all I remember until I felt a stark vibration against my shoulder. Startled, I raised up and realized that it was Doug's pager. He was behind me, sleeping. And I'd fallen asleep too. We had both been so dog tired and so comfortable with each other that we simply crashed! Weren't we a pitiful pair? I reached out and shook Doug hard. "Hey, Casanova, your pager went off."

"Huh? Mmmmm," he said, rubbing his eyes and pressing a button that illuminated the message. It took a couple of seconds for his eyes to focus in order for him to read the pager. "I gotta go, Georgia."

"What's wrong? Is it Butter?"

"No," Doug grunted quickly. "This is another case. Go back to sleep."

Before I could say another word, Doug leaned over and kissed me. When our lips parted, he whispered, "I'll call you as soon as I can. Get some rest."

I was clearly under his spell. My body tried to obey. I heard the door slam and felt myself drifting back into a state of rest. A few seconds later, my eyes popped wide open.

SIXTEEN

*D*oug had lied his butt off.

My instincts, my sixth sense kicked in like a jolt of caffeine. That page Doug took *was* about Butter. He just didn't want to tell me. He wanted to leave me behind in the dark. And I wasn't having it.

Because Doug had only been to my apartment this once, he didn't know about the rear elevator. My building was old and this particular freight elevator could be rigged to go straight to the garage level without stopping on any floor if you pressed all the pop-out buttons on the panel at once. It was a scary trip, like a carnival ride, but a godsend when you're late for work or trying to entertain a feisty nephew like Satch—or aiming to tail a Chicago police detective.

I bolted out of the elevator, ran over to my car, cranked it up, and rolled out of my parking space. I knew what Doug's car looked like and hoped that he wasn't too far ahead. I needed to glimpse enough of him at a distance to follow without too much trouble. Luck was with a sister this night. I spotted Doug up ahead going south on Lake Shore Drive.

Even at this hour, there were a decent number of cars out on Lake Shore Drive as I tailed along after Doug. After a few miles we exited the drive and turned onto a major street that had seen better days. We passed storefronts with their guts hanging out and juke joints with their blues hanging out. We rumbled over railroad tracks and vaulted through viaducts. As late as it was there were still a few people outside on the streets. It was much cooler than it had been during the day, albeit still very warm. The radio station gave weather and time: 83 degrees at 2:30 A.M.

"Where is he going?!" I caught myself asking out loud. We traveled several more miles. I let a light catch me to hide but stay close. Doug turned down a back alley; I couldn't follow, too obvious. I went up one block to a one-way street, hung a left, and sped forward. At the stop sign, I peered to my left and saw Doug's car jetting out of the alley, across the street, and into the next alley. I gunned it and tracked him parallel for two blocks.

My wheels ironed down puffy paper bags and cracked open two-dollar wine bottles as I sped forward, rocking violently over pothole after pothole. I was trying to stay with Doug, but the wear and tear on my Beamer was taking a toll and I whispered "Sorry my man" and petted my steering wheel.

At the third block, Doug turned and headed down a narrow one-way street that led to a set of railroad tracks. I got caught by a red light, waited for a car to pass, then eased forward past the side of one garage painted with a beautiful swirl of reds, blues, and oranges forming the words: Rockies Rule.

The back street led me down the rear of some kind of factory that was pumping an ugly, bruised blue funnel cloud into the air. It smelled like rotten eggs. I almost threw up.

As I rode farther, it seemed as if the stars had decided to pack up their glitter and go to bed. It was incredibly dark, plus now I'd lost sight of Doug's car. I jerked my head left, then right. Where'd he go?

Then I saw his car parked just up ahead of me, partially concealed by a stack of steel drums. The smell was hideous, piercing the window and stitching itself all around the inside of my Beamer. I halted. The car was empty. Where was Doug?

A thunderous rap on my window stopped my heart as my head whipped around.

It was Doug, glaring at me, whirling his right hand in a circular motion and ordering me to roll down my window. I rolled slow and thought fast. I was in trouble with this man, so I tried to play it off. "You scared the stew out of me! And who taught you how to drive—Stevie Wonder?!"

"Don't you try to flip the script with me, Georgia. What are you doing following me, huh?"

"I tried to stay home, Doug."

He rolled his eyes at me.

"Okay, I merely thought about it? That's something isn't it?"

He sucked his teeth.

"That ain't cute," I teased, hoping for some leniency.

Doug growled. "Girl, you're a fool pulling this. You have *no idea* what's going down right now—you're a journalist, not a cop." He paused and looked at me hard, then seemed to soften. "Well, you're here now. And I can't imagine you're gonna sit here and wait for me just because I ask you to. . . ."

I gave him a look that said, Yep you right.

"C'mon then, Georgia. But I'm not playing with you. You do what I say, when I say, and how I say."

"Yes, Doug," I said very soberly. "I understand."

He told me to park behind him. I did. Within two seconds of getting out of my car, sweat was pouring down the back of my neck. It was no secret that my underarms were anything but soft and dry. I had on sandals, sturdy, but still sandals, and they started to feel wet and gooey on my feet. I squinted, looked down, and realized I stood in goo-gobs of black somethin' or other that had the consistency of taffy and smelled like you know what.

"Aaaghhh! Doug, what's this?"

"Who knows? Some kind of waste."

Toxic? Human? "Is this going to make me sick or something?"

"Too late to think about all that now."

I still had no idea where the heck we were. All I could tell was that we were behind some kind of a factory. But that was a lot and a half away now as we walked. We were stepping through all kinds of wet, gooey, oily, sloshy, stinky, gross stuff.

Finally we came upon a pile of garbage the size of Mount Everest. We were in some kind of a waste dump, tucked away on a stretch of back acres in the city. I didn't know it was here and I certainly didn't want to see it up close and personal. Could someone be hiding Butter out here? That poor baby.

I was having problems breathing now from the heat and the smell. My steps got slower and slower. It seemed like he was taking the worst path—he knew I was tired, too. *Doug, how are you gonna play a sister?* I began to take longer strides to keep up; I'd die out here before I'd let him show me up. We stopped behind a cluster of black metal drums stacked two and two just about a foot away from a steep incline. Had we been on a mountain, it would resemble a cliff.

"Why are we stopping?" I whispered.

Doug quieted me before pulling out his gun. He pointed down below us into a flatland crater centered in the dump site. Three cars were parked in a triangle and a fire, burning small and orange, was built off to the side. It gave some presence and a lot of shadow to five men standing around. They had their hands up shoulder high, fists clenched. In the center of them was another person, smaller than all the rest. I couldn't hear what they were saying but all of a sudden they ran to the center and started beating the mess out of the one in the middle.

I decided to call him the Whupped One.

It was rough for the Whupped One. From the

distance the Whupped One looked like he was doing cartwheels. They were kicking and windmilling their arms and he was fighting back, getting up, but each time he got knocked down. They beat him until he was walking drunk. I grabbed Doug's shoulder and said, "Gang ritual. He's getting jumped in."

Doug nodded. "You're dead on."

I'd heard about the practice of beating a new member who joined a gang. I saw a story on one of the networks once where a seventeen-year-old boy had nearly gotten beaten to death by a gang in the Bronx. They interviewed the kid from his hospital bed, and do you know he still said that the gang was his family? He said they loved him. Someone needs to tell these people that love may hurt sometimes but it shouldn't ever require stitches. I told Doug, "They'll kill him."

Doug just shrugged.

"You don't care?"

"He's not part of my posse. I care about me and you, period."

One of the men took a knife and did something to the Whupped One's hand and the rest of them circled around him and embraced each other. The Whupped One could barely stand up.

"Fool," Doug whispered. "Stupid, ignorant fool."

Two of them helped the Whupped One into one of the cars. Two others exchanged a hug and some kind of a shake and one pointed to the fire. The one man left waited until the other cars drove away. Then he began heading up the incline.

"He's coming!"

Doug leaned into my face and blew, "Sssh!"

I tensed. Doug took aim as the man climbed up higher, over the stone-hard garbage as if it were steps. His head was down. He was dressed all in black, with two yellow bandannas tied around his thighs and one around his head. I looked away. My eyes eager for something to do, searched the sky for a seam of light. I found nothing but darkness.

Doug steadied his gun just as Bandanna Man stood up on the edge of the incline.

Hold tight, I thought. Hold tight.

"Represent," Bandanna Man said. Doug had pushed me down and back where I could no longer see much of what was going on.

"The shield is a rock," Doug answered.

"Nothing can shatter the rock," the man responded.

"I got your page. You know where Butter is?"

I held my breath and prayed.

"Naw, man. I keep telling you, I'm not high up like that. But I do have some T for you. Whoever grabbed her is in trouble. They must've been trying to grandstand to get into the top circle but they done fucked up."

"How's that?"

"Whoever snatched her didn't go through security. Never cleared the move. That's enough to get your butt stomped, maybe taken out. Who knows? So nobody will own up to having her. Everybody's edgy, man. They-they think there's another problem, too."

"Shit," Doug said worriedly. "They're not onto you, huh? They think there's a snitch?"

"Yeah, but I'm not talking about our hookup here. We think someone is tippin' our hand to them punk Bandits."

"One of your boys?" Doug asked.

"Yeah, stuff ain't as open as it usta be. We had a meetin' and the chieftains made it clear to the rank and file that whoever had the kid shouldna grabbed her but whoever got her shouldn't hurt her. They put the word out. We don't need that kind of heat. But somethin' is about to go down that might peep where she at. You heard that chick in the hospital faded?"

"Yeah."

"Well, the trouble is bought tight now, and y'all five-oh are about to come down strong on everybody. That's why a move is about to be made. I know for a fact that Little Cap is leaving town tomorrow. We can't afford to hide him out no more now that he's staring down a murder rap."

Little Cap. Finally someone who could at least lead us to the shooter in the drive-by.

"Where is he?" Doug asked.

"Don't know. Just know he leaving town tomorrow sometime. You know Little Cap knows where Butter is. He had to have one of his tight boys hide her, who else would break security and take a chance like that but him and some super-tight partners of his down for theirs? Little Cap is the one with his nuts on the butcher block. You get Little Cap and I believe he'll know where the kid's at."

"I need to know where Little Cap's hiding. I need that info. Get that shit, man!" Doug said, his gruff voice beginning to rise.

"Look, man, I'm takin' a chance tellin' you anything. I ain't 'bout to ask no extra questions and get smoked! I get smoked and then what, huh? Shit, I'm at the crossroads and you still here tryin' to bribe another motherfuckah into being your snitch."

"Chill, just chill, man!" Doug said, trying to placate the rising anger in his informant. "I'm frustrated. I need what I need. If you find out something, I wanna know right away. Understand?"

"If I find out when and where, I'll get to you. For sure. Peace. Hey, don't forget to do that for me like I asked, huh?"

"Okay," Doug said, nodding. Then I saw him crane his neck as the informant walked away.

"I—"

"Sssh!" Doug whispered. "Wait."

I did until I heard the car screech as it pulled off. "This guy has been feeding you inside information?"

"All along. The little information he's provided has helped."

"What kind of a hold do you have on him?"

"Tight. Dude's been in the gang since he was thirteen years old. When you're initiated into their gang, you have to have a sponsor. A big brother. Someone who is responsible for you and your actions until you're grandfathered in after five years of service. His sponsor saved his life on more than one occasion. But now he's in Joliet serving time on assault and drug charges. I'm making sure his time is sweet. Nobody bothers him on the yard and he's got a easy gig in the jail library."

Doug stood up and held out his hand to me as if

he were asking me for a dance. I took his hand and he pulled me up, but I was a little unsteady from lack of sleep and sitting so awkwardly for so long. I stumbled into Doug and he caught me around the waist and squeezed. "Careful, Georgia. Don't get tripped up now. We've got a long way to go together."

SEVENTEEN

*D*oug took me straight home and I crashed. It was my off day. My plan was to sleep until 1:00 P.M., get up to shower, eat, and then throw on some seventies sounds to relax before going to the rally at seven. I told the station that I wasn't about to let anyone else cover the candlelight vigil so I had already hooked it up where a crew would meet me in the neighborhood around 7:30 P.M. so I could set up and cover the story for ten.

It was Zeke's off day, too, and I asked them to call him in on overtime—work half a day but get paid a plus eight at time and a half. I know Zeke. He'll whine but he'll take it. They agreed. I wasn't going to let go of any piece of this story.

That was the plan. Who was it who said the best-laid plans tend to get screwed up? Bad paraphrase but that surely was what I was thinking when my phone rang at 9:30 A.M.

My Caller ID said WJIV-TV.

It was work! I wanted to cry for my mama. Answer it or don't answer it? They could be calling me to pull a double shift on my off day. But I'm beat. Some jobs will work you to death and won't shed a tear or blow snot in a hankie about it. Television news is one such profession. But maybe it was something about Butter? Then maybe it wasn't. I couldn't chance ignoring the call. I answered the phone, putting my head along with the receiver beneath my juicy feather pillow.

"This is Georgia."

"Wake up, Sleeping Beauty!" Clarice said.

"Girl, I'm so tired. I need Z's like I need breath. Let me ring you back, 'kay?"

"No, I need your help, Georgia. I'm in the slot today, running the assignment desk by myself. I need a reporter to come in and turn a package for the noon show."

"Clarice, I'm out on my feet. I was the late reporter last night and you know I've got to cover the rally this evening. Get somebody else."

"Can't. We're vacation heavy and two reporters called in sick."

I groaned; my body ached for more rest. "Who's on call?"

"Brent. And you know he always blows off his page on the weekend, claims he left the pager in his gym bag or his kid was playing with it and turned it off . . ."

"That guy gets away with murder, doesn't he?"

"Girl, it boggles the sane mind. But who needs Brent Manning anyway when I've got you?"

"Sorry, girlfriend, sucking up ain't gonna work this time. Get somebody else."

"Just listen. You've got a leg up on this story. One of the suspects charged with the double homicide in Fellows Park is having a hearing at Twenty-sixth and Cal."

"Which one?"

"Regal Romere. He wants reduced bail."

"So? Who do you know in county jail who doesn't want out? Clarice, that sounds like an anchor voice-over of file tape from the murder scene with a sound bite from Romere's lawyer. Slam-bam and can I get some Z's now, ma'am?"

"No, Georgia! Romere's lawyer says he's got special grounds. If it turns out to be something big and I've got a camera but no reporter on the story, Bing will be in my ass!"

And everyone at WJIV knew what that could be like.

"So you gonna do a solid for me or you gonna leave a sister hanging?"

"Okay, okay!" I threw my pillow away from my head. I had to try to fight it just on principle. "I'm coming, but I turn this bad boy for the noon show only. After that, you have one of the afternoon reporters relieve me on this story. After my live shot, I'm out of there, okay?"

"No problem! That's great, girl."

Twenty-sixth and California Boulevard is where the Cook County Jail and Criminal Courts are located. It's a drab structure, inside and out, and always off temperature. Too hot in the summer. Too cold in the winter. Cameras aren't allowed in the courtrooms. I left my cameraman outside and I went into court. I waved at the station's sketch artist who was sitting in the second row.

Of the two suspects arrested for the double murder in Fellows Park, Regal Romere was the most brazen. He was a chunky man, twenty-one years old, with a hard fade haircut and large, chilly eyes. Satin skin did not hide the hardness of his face. Romere was smirking that day when he was cuffed and walked out of the house, even though his mother stood on the front porch crying into the sleeve of her tattered housecoat.

I hardly recognized him now.

When Romere came into court he looked like hell. His face was drawn and his skin ashy, his eyes were listless and sunken in his head. He'd lost weight and there were bruises on his face worthy of a shot on Showtime Boxing. What happened to him? Who jacked him up?

Romere's lawyer is a cagey joker trying to make a name for himself. Young, fat, balding before his time, the guy had an edge with charm that I'd only seen in successful politicians and up and charging defense lawyers. His name is Gus Wilks.

Wilks told the judge that bond should be reduced from $500,000 to $50,000 because his client's rights had been violated in Cook County Jail. Wilks said that Romere was a diabetic and that he wasn't getting the proper food or sleep because the jail was over-crowded. He also said that Romere had been beaten when he complained to the jail guards.

The state's attorney's office submitted sworn statements that Romere's bruises were from a fight he'd had over food with another inmate. The state's attorney also said the food was standard but Romere was getting his insulin; it was acknowledged that there was overcrowding but Romere did not warrant special treatment. Interesting story but no real bombshell. Most cons screamed abuse; no big deal.

The judge sided with the state. Duh-huh. Reduced bond, denied. Tough guy Romere looked like he needed a box of Puffs tissues. He snatched and yanked at the cuffs on his hands. The guards grabbed Romere's elbows and as he turned around we caught each other's eye. Then Romere did it.

Romere mouthed one word: *Butter.*

I jerked my body forward. Romere didn't say her name again, but he kept staring at me, before nod-ding. I watched them take him away. What did Romere know? How could I get it out of him? I was among three other reporters in the hallway firing questions at Romere's lawyer after court was dis-missed.

I didn't tip anything about what I saw. That was between Romere and me. After I turned my story for the noon, I cornered Romere's lawyer and I told

Wilks I wanted a sit-down with his client now. Wilks hemmed and hawed, and then I told him what Romere had done. Wilks rubbed his chin but he answered too fast for my taste. I think he knows more than he's letting on. I had to be careful. Wilks was nickel slick, as my grandmother would say.

An hour later, I'm sitting down in a room with Wilks, Romere, and my cameraman.

"I know something," Romere said. "If I tell you what I know, can you get me out?"

"I don't know. Tell me where Butter is and—"

"Well, can you get me a cell to myself, huh? Better food?"

"Wait, why are you using me anyway?" I questioned. Was this a setup? Was this a desperate lie to get Romere what he wanted? "Why not cut a deal with the state's attorney's office?"

"Can't trust them to keep their word. You'll be my witness. I'll be on record with you. I tell you first, you tell the cops to get the kid back, and then the state's attorney's office will do right or you blast them on the tube. They don't want that!"

"Aren't you afraid?"

"Fuck the Rockies—punks playing around with a little girl. I got a baby sister. I'm a Bandit and the Bandits got my back. You're my insurance!"

Covering his bet. I swallowed and hoped. "Where is Butter?"

"I don't know exactly—"

I stood up. "I don't have time for this. Play with another reporter."

"Wait!" Romere said, making a motion toward me.

His lawyer grabbed his shoulder. Wilks spoke to me: "Listen to what he has to say."

I sat back down. "What do you know?"

"I overheard two of the Rockies talking. They didn't see me. It's so fucking crowded in there and I was waiting to shower, and I overheard two Rockies—they were high on some homemade liquor snuck in here. They'd just got busted for stealing a Jeep. They said something about 'the package' being too hot to stay in the hiding spot. They said 'it' had to be moved. I've been watching the news. I saw you. I heard about the kid Butter."

"Where do they have her? When did they say they were going to move her?" A break! I heard my heart thumping inside my chest. My mouth got dry.

Romere leaned forward. "You'll help me, right?"

"Yes! Yes! If you're telling the truth—"

"I ain't lying!"

"Where? When?"

"A garage on Sixty-second and Parnell. No exact address. But a garage on Sixty-second and Parnell at two-thirty P.M."

I looked at the clock—it was 1:30 P.M. now! I jumped up and spun on my heels.

"Don't forget! Don't forget!" Romere shouted behind me.

My cameraman grabbed his gear and we headed to Sixty-second and Parnell. I called the cop shop but Doug wasn't there. I told them what was going down. Then I paged Doug twice and got no answer. We were speeding like crazy. I looked at my watch. I looked at the road. My watch. The road. It was 2:00 P.M. We were moving but not like if Zeke had been driving.

Finally we got there and stopped at the opening of an alley and parked. I got out and peeped around the corner. There was a black Chevy parked about three doors down. No squad cars were in sight.

"See anything?" my cameraman asked.

I pointed and he began rolling.

One of the garage doors began to open, and a young man, twenty-something, wearing an oversized football shirt and jeans peeped out. We ducked back. Then I watched him and a teenager dressed in cut-offs and a basketball T-shirt carrying a steamer trunk out of the garage. It's the kind of trunk you packed your clothes in going off to college.

My chest got tight. Where are the police? How can Butter breathe in there? My legs began to tremble. God please, I thought. The older man dropped his end on the ground. It sounded like a cheap fire-cracker as it hit the concrete. I clenched my fist. I heard him curse at the teenager, telling him not to walk so fast. Then he wiped his hands on his back pockets. Two seconds later all hell broke loose.

"Hold it! Hold it!"

Cops were coming from everywhere. From two of the other garages. From the yards catercorner to the trunk. I spotted Doug. The older man dropped his end of the trunk and raised his hands. The teenager went for a gun in his waistband. Doug dived and tackled him around the legs, the teenager hit the ground, and the gun flew out of his hand.

Doug flipped him over. The teenager swung and missed; Doug punched him twice, knocking him unconscious.

"Move! Move!" I spoke over my shoulder and we moved in, slowly rolling the entire time, catching it all on video. "Channel 8 News!" I announced our presence. Some of the officers cursed. Doug looked up at me but he didn't say anything.

The other officers stopped me about three feet from the suspects as they worked to cuff them. The trunk was still on the ground. Then I saw what was leaking out of it.

It was blood.

I stopped, stunned. All my fears burned in my throat and eyes. I opened my mouth and sighed. Doug walked over to me and clutched my shoulder. "You don't want to see this."

One of the officers popped open the trunk, and Doug said, "Turn away."

"Damn!" I heard my cameraman curse. A couple of the cops made comments. What am I going to tell Butter's mother? Her grandmother? And Trip? What kind of anger would be in his heart after this?

"You just butchered the man," I heard one of the cops say.

The teenager shouted, "So what! He smoked our boys in the park!"

"Shut up!" the older suspect shouted. "Don't say nothing, fool!"

The man? I turned and looked quickly when I heard the latch snap back closed. Now the blood was gushing out of the sides of the trunk.

"Doug?" I said, feeling relieved and surprised.

"That's the third suspect in the double murder in Fellows Park. They really hacked him up." Doug looked over at me. "How'd you find out about this anyway?"

"I paged you after I got my tip. Did you get the page?"

"Yeah, couldn't get back to you, obviously. Who tipped you?"

I thought for a second then decided to tell Doug my source; it didn't matter at this point because it was just a fluke anyway. "Regal Romere."

"The Bandit charged with the Fellows Park murders."

"The same, Doug. He's trying to get out of county jail. He overheard snatches of a conversation two Rockies were having. Romere thought the little package they were talking about moving was Butter."

"Huh, that's ironic. That's one of his boys sliced, diced, and Ziploc'ed in that trunk. We'd been looking for him since we arrested Romere and the other suspect. Street talk said he'd made a run to Virginia where his brother lives. My gut kept telling me he was still around somewhere. I just didn't think he was dead in a trunk." Doug scratched his head with a single index finger. "We've got to book these guys. What's next for you?"

"They've got to switch another body out here to finish the coverage. I've got to get some rest for the rally tonight. I want to be fresh for that. I'm going to do a couple of cop interviews here and then run home and fall out."

"Get some rest," Doug said, touching my arm. "You could use it."

Little did I know that in the very next hour there would be a real break in Butter's kidnapping story. That break was just waiting to happen for me back at my apartment.

EIGHTEEN

—

As soon as I walked in the door the message light on my answering machine was flashing fiercely at me. "Yo baby, yo baby, yo!"

I sat on the couch, put the phone next to the takeout food I had stopped to get. I flipped open the pad I keep taped to the phone, grabbed a pencil, and began playing back my messages.

Message #1:

"Georgia, this is Clarice. Got your tape back here. Girl, they messed up that guy in the trunk! Thanks for covering for me. Ron came in and is going to turn that part of the story for us. I know you're tired. Zeke will still meet you at Reverend Walker's church at seven-thirty P.M. for the rally. Zeke might be a little cranky because we told him you specifically requested him. And Zeke said, 'On my off day? Thanks a whole lot!' Sooooo, watch out, girl, he will have his 'tude on. But you're all set, okay? Peace."

Beep!

Message #2:

"Hi, Georgia, it's me."

I hit the stop button—Max's voice made my heart jump. Why was he calling? We had broken up and he refused to return my calls. Now out of the blue he phones? I thought of the slant of his mouth when he laughed, the glow of his gold-nugget eyes, his soft hair, slim body, and the way his mind became a speedway when he was working angles to a breaking story.

I pressed the play button again.

". . . ran into old Liz here in Washington covering a story, she asked about you. I said you were fine and gave her your phone number. That's all, bye."

That's all. Just like Max to call and not even say hope you're doing well. A night of passionate lovemaking flashed through my mind. I doubled forward—willing myself not to call Max back or think about him another second!

Beep!

Message #3:

"Georgia, this is Mom. Well, Ms-I've-got-a-secret. Your sister tells me this man you were with at the Blues Box is a police detective. I don't know if I like that at all. You'll be constantly worried about something happening to him. But Peaches says he's awful handsome—"

"I said he fine, sister-twin! Ma, quote me right if

176

you're gonna tell what I told you after you said you wouldn't!"

"—Be quiet, girl, whose fault is it that you can't keep a secret? I'm the mother and I can do what I want. Georgia? Call your mama dear. Bye."

Beep!

Message #4:

"What a long beep! Georgia, this is Carmen at the phone company. I've got that information you wanted on that call made to your apartment the other morning. The call came from 50-23 South Hedge. The phone is registered in the name of Viola Martin. That's 50-23 South Hedge, registered in the name of Viola Martin. I got this straight from the researcher handling the police request. He hasn't called them yet—went to lunch—so you've got it first! Talk to you later, bye!"

Viola Martin, 50-23 South Hedge? I hit the rewind button on the answering machine again: ". . . came from 50-23 South Hedge. The phone is registered in the name of Viola Martin. . . ." I pressed the stop button, shoved the white plastic fork in my mouth, and left it there to bob around as I chewed. I got up and grabbed my reporter's notebook.

I found it, flipped back through the pages, chewing awkwardly with the fork still in my mouth, searching until I came to my notes at the hospital. The old lady at the table . . . Auntie Vee . . . yes, that was the name I had scribbled and Jason Martin gave me the family's address of 50-23 South Hedge.

The ransom call came from the Martins' house—

the family of the young girl who died in the drive-by shooting.

I hit the showers. It was my second shower of the day, not because the humidity had made my clothes bunch up like satin sheets against my behind, but because water helped me to think. The warm rush of liquid soaked my skin and released from it the stress of the past few days. The stress seemed to ooze from parts of my body, blowing water bubbles that beaded on the edge of my collarbone, on the tip of my nipples, and on the cuticles of my fingers. I was trying to relax and deal with this latest development.

Now I knew that my early morning ransom call had definitely come from the Martins' house. My mind could now only settle on one person. One suspect.

Jason.

Was it his voice on the phone?

I had struggled to etch the telephone voice onto the slack reel of tape in my brain; at the time it was being tugged at by the tension of Butter's disappearance and the excitement of possibly finding her.

When I tried to match that voice from the phone with that of the man who met me beneath the el tracks, I was sure they were one and the same.

But was it Jason's voice? Had time and stress dulled my senses so Jason didn't sound familiar when I met him in the hospital? I could easily have missed the connection because I wasn't looking for it. His voice was deep enough. But people can alter their voices, too. Was it Jason I was after?

Jason said he left town before the gangs could jump him in. Did he? Doug had mentioned that once you're in a gang you're in for life. Maybe they jumped Jason in and his family sent him away after he got into trouble? What did Jason know about Butter's disappearance? Could he help us find her?

I threw on my lightest weight clothing, got in my car, and drove like the Zeke over to the Martin house. I was going to ask plenty of tough questions. I also needed to beat it there before the police—especially Doug, who had been tying my hands on this story quite a bit lately.

The house at 50-23 South Hedge was four doors down from Butter's place. Each house on the block was constructed the same, from white wood frame. Families tried to distinguish their homes by painting the borders of the windows different colors, from candy red to royal blue to banana yellow.

The Martin house was painted steel gray. Shiny wicker baskets hung from hooks drilled into the overhang that provided a patch of shade the width and length of a giant envelope. The flowers inside the baskets had pooped out, losing their vibrant colors to a battered brown because of the heat wave that was now, thank God, subsiding.

The front door of the Martin house was open behind the protective mesh of a silver screen door that was buff taut at the top and beer gut at the bottom. I could hear a bunch of people chatting and moving around inside the house. I rang the doorbell and an elderly man sitting by the door leaned out and around, peering at me from behind low-on-the-nose glasses. He reached up to unfasten the screen door. His fingers looked old, tight, and stuck together, and they couldn't flick the tiny button beneath the handle.

"Hey," he yelled. "One of y'all kids come unfasten this door here, shoot."

I saw Jason Martin come snoop-footing toward the door. He opened the screen, stepped up, and partly closed the wooden door behind him.

"Jason, I need to talk to you."

"Please," he said firmly, his eyes bloodshot and puffy. "The family . . . we really don't feel like talking. All the other television stations came here with cameras and stuff. We turned them all away. Really, we just want to be to ourselves for a while."

"Jason, as you can see I don't have a crew with me."

"Then why are you here?"

"I'm here for another reason, an important reason that can't wait another second."

"Look, I don't want to get into anything—"

"You're already in it and if I were you I'd give me some time."

"In what?" Jason's face took on a hard edge to it. "And what do you mean 'if I were you'?"

"I mean I need to talk to you somewhere a little more private. It's important. I want to talk to you before the police do."

"*Police?* They aren't coming here."

"I promise you they are."

"For what?"

"That's what you're going to tell me."

I was deliberately baiting him. I wanted to see if I could find a crack. Did he know something and was acting out the nut role? If he was acting, and Jason very well could be, how long could he dance around stage with the heat steadily being turned up. Turned up by me.

Jason stepped out onto the porch, his eyes narrowing with suspicion. He turned and pointed at a junky sofa that was smashed up against an outside wall. I sat down in the middle. Jason sat down on the edge.

I slid over. I wanted to be close enough to read his body language, voice change, anything and everything I could when I questioned him.

"What's so important that you've gotta dis me on my own property?"

I do understand his anger, but I wasn't afraid of it and, to be butt-naked honest, I didn't give-a-care! Not right now. Butter was still missing and the first link I had to where she might be was sitting next to me on a couch full of fuzz balls.

"I got a call from a man a couple of nights ago asking for money. It was about four o'clock in the morning—"

"I don't wanna hear about your love life." Jason smirked.

"You're not cute."

"And you're not making sense," he said, getting up. "I'm gone . . ."

"Well." I shrugged. "I'll just wait until the police get here and let them ask the questions."

Jason sat back down.

"As I was explaining, the caller said he would tell me where Butter was. I took a thousand dollars of my own hard-earned money and met him up under an el track—he damn near broke my arm taking the money—and almost got shot by police who tried to run him down, but he got away."

"Cops can't catch a brother."

"But he never said where Butter was. He showed me a piece of her dress—but never said where she was."

Jason looked at me with a stare that was empty of emotion, even of interest. What was the deal? Was Jason just drained of feeling because of the sudden loss of his sister? Was Jason completely ignorant of the entire situation? Or maybe he knew something and was holding back.

"Guess where the ransom call to my apartment came from?" I asked.

"I'm not in a guessing mood."

"The call came from your house."

"From here? Can't be," Jason said with a mix of indignation and disbelief. "From here?"

"That's right."

"It's a mistake. Gotta be a mistake," Jason said, moving forward to lean on his elbows. "We don't know nothing about where Butter is."

"The police think you do."

"Aww nah. See, I smell some shit. What are you trying to say?"

"I'm not trying to say anything; I'm trying to hear what you have to say."

"I don't need this bullshit! And my sister just

got killed, too? You must be crazy or something."

"Someone in this house knows something, Jason—the trace is no mistake. Who could have made the call?"

"Nobody was even here!"

"Baby? What's wrong out there?" an elderly woman called out from inside the house.

"Nothing, Auntie Vee," Jason said soothingly to her, but looking pretty darn hateful at me. "There's somebody out here trying to sell me some junk is all."

"Don't buy it!" she warned.

"I'm not buying it!"

"Jason, you can help me figure it out or you can talk to the police. We both know how funky the police can get."

"Is that a threat?"

"No, that's info. The police have been getting a potful of bad publicity on this case. They want to close it and fast so they'll come down extra hard on anyone they even think is connected to it."

"No one was home, don't you understand?" Jason put his head in his hands. "We all spent the night in the hospital. Everybody. We didn't leave."

"Jason, it looks funky, man."

"Naw, you're the funky one. This is a setup. Nobody was here—"

Jason stopped in mid-sentence, like a bad video on pause. His voice was lost in a hollow space deep in his chest and his face was stuck on blank.

"What is it, Jason?"

Jason's face stayed stuck on blank.

"Listen," I said, borrowing the tone I used when I talked to my nephew Satch, "it doesn't make sense to protect anyone because it will only come out eventually. Your family's hurt will only be doubled, but if you help me get Butter back safe then I'll do all I can to help you and your family."

I heard him breathe and saw him blink. Jason stood, leaned up against the screen door, and pinched the bridge of his nose with long fingers, chewed albino white around the nails. "He wouldn't grab a little kid. He's not that kind of guy."

"He who? Who is he?" I stood up and jerked Jason's hand down from his face.

"Just—just leave me alone, huh! I don't need this," Jason said, turning his face away from me.

"Like Butter's family does? Like I do? There's a little girl out there somewhere and no one seems to know where and I'm tired of this whole mess and I want it over with. How about you?"

"Yeah."

"Not *yeah*, Jason, who?"

"Calvin Hughes."

"Calvin Hughes? Who is Calvin Hughes?"

Jason spoke slowly, as if he had just awakened from a deep sleep. "He's a neighbor. Calvin stayed in our house a couple of nights."

"Why?"

"Big Cal was just watching things. Sometimes folks will hear that you're gone and try to rip you off."

"Was it your idea or his idea to stay at the house?"

"Auntie Vee thought it would be a good idea for a couple of nights to have Big Cal stay over. Our families have known each other for years. Been on the block together for ages. His cousin Karen was sitting out with Jackie and T-Bob when the drive-by went down."

"Wait." My mind was trying to put together a picture in my head. "Is Big Cal a tall guy around forty, gray at the temples?"

"Uh-huh."

Calvin Hughes was the man I had interviewed at the drive-by. He was comforting his young cousin Karen at the scene. It's funny how for a reporter people start to either blend together or they stay with you forever. There are days when I can't remember the name of a city alderman not ten minutes after doing a sit-down interview on some political issue. Then there are days when I see something, a car smashed up and smoldering from a wreck, or a jet doing a loopdie-lu at the Air and Water Show, or a line at the Pacific Garden Mission on Christmas Eve and the image stays with me forever. Like now, I saw Calvin Hughes, and this second time around, details from our first meeting came to me.

I remember his close-cropped hair and the gray at the temples.

I remember the muscular arms, the grime of a working man beneath his fingernails.

I remember the anger from his eyes and the tenderness with which he stroked and consoled his crying cousin. I got all that as I listened to Jason fill in more details.

"Big Cal has a garage over on Forty-seventh but I can't believe he's mixed up in this Butter business."

"Why?"

"He has always been one of the straight ones on the block—no gangbanging or nothing."

"But what made Big Cal act like he had some sense and turn his back on gangbanging?"

"Football."

"Pro?"

"College. He could have been pro. Big Cal would have gone pro for sure had he not busted his hip his second year in college. They yanked his scholarship but Big Cal was always good with his hands. He can fix anything. When Big Cal opened his garage he gave jobs to a couple of the guys in the neighborhood who are good mechanics, too. In the summer he lets the teenagers pump gas or the girls work the counter. Jackie and Karen both worked for him."

"Where can I find Mr. Hughes?"

NINETEEN

———

Jason took me to the garage Calvin Hughes owned, Driven Auto Works. It was a blunt building, gangster leaning to the right. The reddish-orange brick needed a good cleaning. Next to the building was a lot filled with an assortment of parts: bumpers and tires, doors and windshields, headlights and rearview mirrors, even a row of mix-and-match oval bucket seats from the retro Volkswagen days.

There was also an old Camaro, valentine red, sitting propped up on double cinder blocks. I love the old seventies Camaro. It's still the sexiest car I've ever seen. Every Negro in America and overseas looked good driving a red Camaro; it was the car where I got my first tongue kiss on a summer-breeze night. And I remember that Peaches said that she felt the kiss, too, way back home as she pouted in bed, grounded for having too much mouth.

There were two gas pumps out front, and through the window you could see a seating area, a counter, and two desks sitting behind the counter next to a row of file cabinets. Calvin Hughes was leaning over a young lady's shoulder going over some papers. She looked like the girl he was comforting at the drive-by. Jason confirmed this fact with his greeting.

"Hey, Big Cal," Jason said as we walked through the door. "Hey, Karen."

Calvin smiled at him and his eyebrows went up when he saw me. Was it just surprise or fear? I wondered.

"Hello, Mr. Hughes. I'm Georgia Barnett, Channel 8. I interviewed you, the day of the drive-by."

"Right," Calvin said, meeting us at the counter and leaning over to shake my hand. Then he cuffed Jason around the neck. "Sorry about Jackie, man. Really. How's the rest of the family?"

"Holding up, man—just barely holding up," Jason said, and the sorrow of the situation started to come down on him. His body slumped over the counter and he dropped his eyes and all at once I felt very bad for him.

"Be strong, man," Calvin said to Jason. "You've got to take the lead in the family and be strong."

I exchanged glances with Karen, Calvin's teenage cousin, who was almost a shooting victim in the drive-by earlier this week. She gave me a smile as genuine as a strand of fake pearls. I turned my attention back to Calvin and Jason. "Jason, do you want to tell Calvin why I'm here?"

Jason dropped his eyes and looked away. "Naw, you."

Calvin looked from Jason to me and back again. "What's up?"

"Thursday morning around four A.M. I got a call at my house from a man demanding money for information about Butter. I took a thousand dollars to the guy under the el tracks on Sixty-third but he got spooked, took some of the money, and got away. That call to my apartment came from Jason's house."

Reporters learn to watch people's faces for reactions, to get a sense of what's going on inside. Calvin's brow wrinkled and his eyes softened and he looked at Jason. "Man, I know you're not mixed up in something like that, huh?"

"Not me," Jason said, and he looked Calvin straight in the eye.

Calvin shrugged at me. "What then? I don't get it."

"Jason and his family were at the hospital at the time the call was made. You, however, were at the house the night the call was made."

"What?" Calvin said, rearing back. He made two fists, planted them on the counter, and leaned forward. "What are you trying to say, lady?"

"Just the truth," I told him. "Now add this. I gave you my card with my home number on the back after I interviewed you at the drive-by scene. You had the number and access to the phone that the call was made from."

"I don't even know what I did with the card,

probably threw it away. You think I would do something to hurt a little kid?" Calvin was leaning over the counter now pointing an angry finger in Jason's face. "Jason, you ought to know better than this, man. Why would you bring some mess down on me like this?"

"Cal, I know that. It's not me, it's her!" Jason said, directing his anger at me.

Now they were both snorting in my direction. I stood my ground like a bullfighter, continuing to wave the facts at Calvin. "The call came from the Martins' house. If Jason didn't make the call, and you didn't make the call, who did? Somebody is lying because one of you knows something."

With my peripheral vision, I could see Karen nervously cutting her eyes down at the papers on the desk, then back up in our direction.

I got louder. "Do you both want to go to jail? The police are something like two seconds behind me on this one, but if you'll just tell me what the deal is and help me find Butter, I'll do what I can for you."

Now Karen's hands were shaking and the paper was making sharp rustling noises.

"Was there anyone else in the house with you?" I asked Calvin.

"Just me and my cousin so I know this is just some kind of crazy mix-up!" Karen dropped the papers she had been reading and began to cry. She cupped her hands to her face and the tears dripped out from a tiny gap near the edges of her wrists.

Calvin rushed over to Karen and tried to stand her up, but she was limp. "What's wrong?"

I had an idea. I hadn't thought of it until Karen

began to get nervous. I comforted her, saying, "Calvin didn't make the call, did he? Jason didn't either. Karen, you found my card and gave it to someone. That someone made the call."

She stopped crying long enough to stutter, "T-T-T . . ."

"T-Bob!" Calvin shouted and slammed the heel of his palm against a bad spot in the wall. A hollow sound burst out. Calvin wiped his hand across his entire face from his forehead down to his chin. He struggled with his hurt feelings. Calvin clasped his hands together tightly, then his words hissed from his lips, "Karen, you snuck T-Bob in the house?"

"We weren't doing nothing, just being together. I had to sneak him in. You know you can't stand T-Bob."

"You see why now, don't you?" Calvin's voice rose. "Look at the shit he's mixed up in."

Karen tried to explain. "T-Bob said he didn't know where Butter was but that he could pretend like he did and talk his way into some easy money. T-Bob said TV people make a lot of bank and she wouldn't even miss it. T-Bob was gonna buy us matching Sky Walker shoes. All he had to do was go get the money and run."

"Well, now T-Bob is in deep trouble and so are you," I told Karen. "The police are going to come down hard on anyone connected to this crime."

"I'm sorry. I swear. Here, I got most of the money, I'll give it back. Here!" She reached down in her purse and pulled out three crumpled one-hundred-dollar bills.

"Let me see those," I said, and Calvin unhooked the hip-high swinging door of the counter. Jason followed and stood behind me as I took the money and looked at it. They all had my mark—the *In* whited out, leaving "God We Trust." "This is the money I gave him, all right."

"Karen," Calvin yelled, "how could you be in on something that low-down and stupid? I work like a dog for our family. I buy you damn near everything you ask for!" Calvin was pacing, his words stumbled past his lips he was blurting them out so quickly. "Can't believe this. It's crazy! Damn! This is trouble! Trouble!"

Karen was trembling and the motion sent tears flying. "You don't wanna hardly let me do nothing! T-Bob can't hardly come around. I love T-Bob. But, he—he wouldn't hurt a little girl. He wouldn't!"

Calvin grabbed Karen and started to shake her violently. Karen's open mouth made this guttural waah sound just like when you shook one of those big old-fashioned dolls I used to play with—and Peaches used to tear up—as a kid. "Are you crazy? Are you crazy?!" Calvin screamed.

Jason grabbed one of Cal's arms and I grabbed the other. It was like trying to move a jungle gym, his arms were just that solid.

"Calvin, stop it!" I yelled.

I felt myself being moved aside from behind. It was Doug. He shoved Jason out of the way, too. Jason fell backward, both elbows whacking against the top of the counter. Doug then grabbed Calvin in a headlock, pinned one of his arms behind his head, and smashed his face up against the wall. "Break it up!"

"Bastard!" Calvin grunted, saliva dripping out of his mouth.

"Let him go!" Karen screamed. "Let him go!"

"I will," Doug announced calmly to the room, "but he has to get himself in check." As Calvin's breathing became more even, Doug applied less body pressure. "Thank you. Now be cool, man, because I'm going to ease up off you." Slowly Doug backed away. Calvin jerked around and raked Doug with his eyes from the top of his head down to the tops of his shoes.

I stepped in and explained everything to Doug. As it turned out, he had gone to the Martin house after getting back the information on the phone call. The old guy sitting by the door had overheard Jason talking about Calvin and told him where the garage was.

Doug spoke firmly to Karen. "If you don't want to be charged as an accomplice you'd better tell me where T-Bob is."

"Hey, ease up, brah-thar!" Calvin said angrily. The veins around his temples pulsed in direct sync with the fierceness of his words. "Karen's just a kid! You damn cops are mean, you don't think about anybody but yourselves. You're just an Uncle Tom Negro doing the white man's work!"

Doug stiffened as if a bolt of lightning had struck him and an intense anger radiated from his body, seeping like poison from his eyes. He swallowed before unleashing his response.

"If people in the neighborhoods would stop taking all this shit from the gangs and get together and
say *no,* and help us, then we could get these motherfuckers up out of here. But nooooooo, *you'd* rather
protect a punk like T-Bob . . . who you think is *all
right* when he *ain't* . . . than to *help* somebody like me
who'll come to your rescue and put his life on the
line! Regularly I get shot at, cussed out, spit on,
ridiculed by the media. And, every solar eclipse,
thanked by *some* somebody with sense. Does anybody, I said, does any-*some*-body want to walk in my
shoes *today?*"

That shut us all up swift and in a hurry.

"Now!" Doug turned to Karen. "I'll ask you
again, and for the last time, do you know where
T-Bob is?"

TWENTY

She did and she told.

T-Bob was part of a basketball league playing at an outdoor court at the Elder Housing Projects about three miles west of the gas station. We had to wait until a squad car came to take Calvin and Karen down to the station; another detective working the case would take their statements. While Doug talked to them, I excused myself and headed for the bathroom in the rear where I had spotted a pay phone. I called my television station, gave them an address, and told them I needed a crew to meet me. Doug would be mad when he found out, but I'd deal with that when the time came.

When the other officers arrived, Doug once again attempted to ditch me. But this time the discussion was much shorter because we both knew it just wasn't going to happen. When we got in Doug's car, he called for backup to meet us at the basketball court. He would go in first, then cue them to come in just in case the crowd or T-Bob and his friends got any funky ideas.

"I want to make sure there's no chance on this earth that my man T-Bob will get away," Doug said. "He's got too much knowledge and he's gonna give it up whether he wants to or not."

"You've got something big on him?"

"Georgia, I'm not just banking on your testimony. I got back the prints taken at the el tracks the night you had your own little personal meeting with the ransom caller. The prints came up Tyrell Robert Adams. T-Bob."

I appreciated the fact that Doug was being honest and real with me. He was direct. Up front. He could be extremely calm or explosive with energy. He was a take-charge guy. I was finding myself fiercely attracted to this man. I wanted to jump this guy's bones. But are they the kind of bones I want to jump and keep or just jump and bury?

"So what are you thinking about?" Doug asked.

"The case. Butter. What happened at Driven Auto Works," I said, slow dancing my way to the subject. "You got pretty fiery back there, Mr. Doug."

"Georgia," he said easily, "let me tell you, that was nothing. I was juiced but that wasn't even my most hyped level. How do you think I survive out here? Had I pampered that girl back there she'd a lied through her teeth, and her cousin too, honest though he seems to be, because people in the hood

196

don't like cops. But they hate crime, too. Now go figure that ass-backwards logic. How are you going to
hate crime and then hate the very people who can
get rid of it for you? There's this minus-minus thing
happening and they're canceling each other out.
That leaves things the same—plain old *bad.*"

"I'm not trying to judge you, Doug, because I
don't want you judging me."

"That's good, Georgia, because people have to
accept others as they are to develop any kind of relationship, whatever it is—romantic, friendship, or
working. No one likes to be judged, so they shouldn't
do it to anyone else."

I agreed. Then Doug looked back up ahead. Just
beyond the red light we'd come to, I could see the
basketball court in the distance. The crowd was
dense, partly because it was the first reasonably cool
evening that we'd had in a week. The sun had gone
from a festering blister to a smooth, waxy palette of
warmth and color.

It was a game of Cut-Off Red T's versus Skins.

The Skins were likely the most comfortable, their
sepia tones made shiny by the sweat dripping off
their backs. We were sitting in the car across the
street, on an angle, watching. The athletics were
stunning; with a step, one of the young men would
vamoose into the air and slam-dunk in gravity's face.
The crowd cheered and it seemed as if there were no
clear sides for or against, just appreciation for talent.

I struggled to pick out T-Bob. Dap-gum-it,
where's that boy? Karen had given us a photo of him;
it was the kind of picture kids and adults in love, or

in deep like, tend to take. It was a picture of a couple squeezed into one of those photo booths in the mall.

T-Bob's face was the color of Concord grapes, as much of it as could be seen. Only about half was showing behind Karen's head as she sat in his lap, her mouth turned up in a cheesy smile. T-Bob's expression was pleasant but stony and he had his right arm looped around Karen's neck hugging her close, making some kind of gang sign with his hands.

"There's the backup," Doug said as he stopped the car. He nodded to an unmarked car parked catercorner to us. Then he pointed a thumb sideways across the street at a black guy in sneakers and jeans standing in the doorway of a liquor store. A block down from him was a paddy wagon easing into a parking space behind a truck where a guy was stacking up boxes of potato chips for delivery.

Doug turned to me and said, "Stay here."

"And miss all the action?"

"You are so hardheaded." Doug moaned in an exasperated manner.

That didn't sit with me at all. "Determined," I said, substituting a word I deemed more fitting.

Doug blew a sigh, then gave me a wry smile. "Georgia, stay about ten feet behind me. When I get on the outside of the fence, I'll scout him out on the court. Once there's a break in the action—a time-out or foul—I'm going to make my move. Stay put behind the stands. The kids are likely to start yelling and throwing stuff. You don't want to get knocked in the head."

I agreed and I let Doug move out first. I followed ten paces behind. I tried to look cool and I did, even putting on my shades and walking like I was just out chilling. But who was looking across the street anyway? Everyone was watching the court.

Doug stopped at the gate entrance, which was open, and leaned against a metal pole. I was looking through the fence in between spectators who jumped up and sat down, cheered and hooted, ooohed and aahed. *Where's T-Bob?*

The action stopped.

I was getting more and more nervous as I watched Doug raise his hand overhead to signal the cop across the street.

I finally spotted T-Bob. He was at the free throw line. He bent his knees and was leaning on them with the palms of his hands, pulling his black shorts way down. T-Bob let the sweat drip off his brow onto the court, marking his territory, before he glanced up.

That's when he saw Doug making his move.

I caught it in T-Bob's eyes, that speck of panic. T-Bob looked behind him quickly. What was he looking at? My eyes darted hard. Left. Right. I was trying to find it, whatever T-Bob saw. Then I glimpsed a hole in the fence where there were no benches, a narrow opening where two sets of bleachers almost but didn't quite connect.

Doug was moving closer. I couldn't tell if he knew T-Bob had spotted him. Should I yell? That might set the crowd off or throw Doug off-balance. I made a move myself. I eased around the side of the fence.

T-Bob took the ball from the ref and started to

bounce it. Doug was getting closer when someone in the crowd yelled, "Who is that?"

I was running around the fence now.

"Tyrell Robert Adams?" Doug said, pulling out his badge holding it high, eye level.

T-Bob took the ball and snapped it right in Doug's face.

Doug went down, grabbing his nose and rolling over and over on the court. T-Bob took off running for the gap in the fence that meant a chance to escape.

But I was running for it, too. T-Bob is probably twice as fast as me but I had a head start. I heard the kids in the stands yelling, "Run! Run!"

Cops were running onto the court. One knelt over Doug and three more ran after T-Bob. As soon as he hit that hole in the fence, I was about three steps away. I slipped my purse off my shoulder just as T-Bob turned sideways to slide through that gap. I slung my purse at his ankles. T-Bob tripped. He fell flat on his face, panting against the ground. I put my knee in his back and two fingers at the back of his head and said in a Get Christie Love voice, "Freeze!"

T-Bob froze. Jeez, that crap actually worked?

I could feel sweat running down the back of my neck, afraid that any second he would turn around. God, please don't let this boy turn his head around and see how I was bs-ing him with my fingers.

One of the cops came and pushed me out of the way. "Got him!" he said. The cop's gun was drawn and he swapped it for my fingers, placing the barrel at the back of T-Bob's head. "Who the hell are you?"

the cop said to me without letting his eyes leave the young black teenager sprawled in front of him.

T-Bob moved.

"Cough, motherfucker! Please cough so I can blow your brains out!" the cop shouted, nudging his skull with the gun.

"I'm Georgia Barnett, Channel 8 News."

"Damn!" T-Bob shouted into the ground. Then shaking his head, he said, "What I do? What y'all want?"

TWENTY-ONE

You helped kidnap Butter and we want to know where she is," I told T-Bob as the cop jerked him to his feet.

"Hey, we gonna be on TV!" one of the teenagers in the stands yelled out, pointing.

I looked across the court and saw a crew from my station shooting video of the scene. The truck was on the blind side of the court. I waved as Al, one of the ace cameramen at the station, started running toward me.

My little secret of phoning for a crew at the repair shop was now as public as a rip in a pair of fishnet stockings. I wasn't about to miss getting this exclusive.

Al got as close as the cops would let him. He shot b-roll as we crossed the court with T-Bob cuffed and head bowed. The kids were booing and hissing; one of them threw a can at the cop. We both ducked behind T-Bob, shamelessly using the boy as a shield.

Doug was now sitting up holding a big, white towel against his nose. He saw the cameraman and our eyes met. Doug shrugged, realizing I had tipped my station off. We followed the cop to the squad car where he put T-Bob in the backseat.

My cameraman got a shot of T-Bob in the back of the car. Doug came over to the vehicle. "Georgia, lose the camera now!" he said firmly.

"Doug, be cool, okay?"

"I am cool, just lose the camera."

The cameraman kept rolling on T-Bob in the back of the squad car. Doug waved his hand disgustedly in the direction of my cameraman, then he bolted around to the driver's side of the squad car, opened the door, and slid in. I got in the front passenger side. "Doug, we're just doing our job here, okay?"

"Well, quit it for a second and let me do mine!"

I waved Al away and he began shooting video of the basketball court itself.

Doug ignored my gesture of peace and started in on T-Bob. "Man, do you know you damn near broke my nose?"

T-Bob was staring at the dashboard.

"You're quiet now, huh? That's assault and battery against a police officer *plus* kidnapping *and* child endangerment for snatching Butter."

T-Bob ignored both of us, continuing to perfect his glassy-eyed stare at the dashboard.

"I wonder how quiet you'll be when we throw your punk ass in a cell, making sure that when you go up—and you will go up—that your first month is in the hole. It's hot. It stinks. There's no light at all. . . ."

T-Bob didn't turn his head, he just said, "So what? Night never ends."

"Doug, he said that to me at the el tracks!" The voice was the same, too.

Doug explained, "That's a sign for his gang. Just like some gangs have a handshake to represent, they can represent verbally. Their code is: Night never ends."

"The Rockies," I assumed, the gang that had Butter and was led by Little Cap.

T-Bob jerked his head and looked at me. "Naw, Bandits rule!"

"Bandits? How could that be?" I asked Doug. "Butter described a Rockie—a dark-skinned gang-banger with a scar, wearing the Rockies' color yellow. The shooter, you said, was Little Cap."

"Right, Georgia. But this sounds like the Bandits took it upon themselves to hide Butter to keep the Rockies from getting their hands on her. But why? Why not turn her over to us to make some points? Or cut a deal? Are you guys so low-down that you held on to that kid just to keep the Rockies in hot water with us? You wanted us to keep riding them, coming down hard on them? What's the deal, T-Bob?"

T-Bob still didn't say anything. *Now this nut gets shy, please.*

"Doug, you've been holding out on me."

He stared at me and smiled. "Not long. I had a hint that something wasn't quite on the up-and-up when my source couldn't get a lead for me. Then when I saw the picture of T-Bob and Karen and Romeo here was flashing his gang sign in that photo—it's the Bandits' sign."

I sat back against the car seat and an exasperated sigh left my lips.

"T-Bob, we need answers *now*," Doug said, then he reached back over the car seat and grabbed T-Bob by the neck and yanked his face toward him.

"I don't know where she at!" T-Bob shouted, spittle flying off his lips.

"Son, there is no joy in Stateville," Doug said, releasing him to let him ease down in the seat, "and you may not get much romance now, but behind bars you a fine young thang."

"I don't know where she at, broke-nose motherfucker!"

Doug slammed his face into the back of my seat. "Punk!"

"Damn! Awww!" T-Bob moaned.

"Take it easy, Doug! Don't be an animal like him!"

A hurt look filled Doug's eyes.

"I didn't mean that . . ."

"Georgia, this is my territory. Let me handle my business. This punk pimped you out of your money. The gang he runs with tried to kill Little Cap's mother by firebombing her house. You were there. You could have been a Cocoa Krispy if that fire had gotten out of hand. And he knows where Butter is—"

"I don't!"

"Shut up!" Doug said to T-Bob. Then to me, "And you want me to go easy? Explain to me why the hell I should?"

I was speechless.

T-Bob shouted, "I don't know nothin'!"

"Then where'd you get that piece of Butter's dress from?" I asked.

"I got it from the brother who hid her. He know. He ain't tell nobody else in case there was a snitch somewhere. He ain't tell nobody, not even me!"

"Who the hell is 'he'?" Doug said, dropping his fist.

"You gonna cut me a deal, huh, cut me some slack?" T-Bob said, showing the first sign of weakness.

"Yeah, my word, man."

"Fuck that, I want it wrote down somewhere," T-Bob said, shaking his head hard and fast.

"My word is my word, we don't have time for all that. Maybe I'll just take my chances and keep digging and turn this case by myself without your punk ass!"

"Naw, man. You'll try to play me," T-Bob said.

"He won't T-Bob," I said, trying to coax him. "Make it easy on yourself and let's just end this thing."

"She's right," Doug said with a nod. "And she'll keep me honest."

T-Bob looked from Doug to me, then back to Doug. He whispered, "Trip, Butter's cousin. He know where Butter at."

My head fell into my hands. "Trip?"

"Y'all are grabbing them out of the cradle now, huh?" Doug said.

"Little man come to us right after that drive-by. We had been talking to him before but he didn't want to join. We finally convinced Trip that it was the best way to protect his family. He got a family of females and he the only man—"

"Man?" I shouted. "Trip is a kid, just a baby!"

"Trip needs family like us to look out for him. I'm his sponsor—I vouched for him, advise and protect him."

I became mesmerized by the urgency and the calmness of T-Bob's voice; the matter-of-fact manner in which he spoke of handicapped codes and manufactured rules that kept both order and violence in his world.

"When word spread that Butter had told it on TV, then turned up missing, everybody thought the Rockies had her. But only me and Trip knew different."

"Why tell you?" Doug asked. "Why not keep the secret to himself?"

"'Cause he was scared, wasn't sure he had done the right thing. I'm his sponsor, he's supposed to confide in me, bringing everything to me first. That's the rules of the Bandits. I didn't believe him at first, I thought he was lying and wasting my time. Told him to prove it. Next time I saw him, he had part of her dress. I took it, then kicked his ass."

"Why?" I asked.

"Because he shouldn't made no move like that

without coming to me first, then letting me take it to the council. I vouched for him. Trip broke rules and that could get us both in a lot of trouble. Trip wouldn't tell me where she was, so I told him just sit tight until things cooled down some. Hell, it was sweet now that you think about it. Trip could protect his cousin and fuck over the Rockies at the same time."

"And you could exhort some cash too, huh," Doug said with a smirk.

"After I saw all the TV coverage, I got the idea to squeeze some money out of old girl here—"

"You little son-of-a-bitch," I huffed.

"Keep talking, T-Bob!" Doug warned.

"Trip gave me a piece of Butter's dress but I had nothing to do with her *ever.*"

"This is insane."

Doug whispered, "Now all we have to do is find Trip."

"Trip on a mission," T-Bob said. "See how much I'm helping you? You gotta give back, man, that's the rules of the street."

"I hear you."

"What kind of a mission?" I asked.

"A monster mission, hip-hyped style."

"Look, boy," I said to T-Bob. "Explain to me in the ways of Webster—just talk in simple English please."

"Trip too little to get jumped in like everybody else. That's too much of a beating for a little dude to take. So he got a mission to do to prove he's worthy of the Bandits."

208

Doug grunted. "A death mission."

I sighed. "Ohhhh no!"

"Trip know he can't hide Butter forever. The only way Butter can come out of hiding is if Little Cap— the one who did the firing at the drive-by—gets smoked. He gone. Then what Butter know ain't important no more. Everything is cool, plus Trip has proved himself and he in. So he gotta smoke somebody stogie."

"Stogie." Doug turned and explained to me. "Like the cigar. Big and high profile. Like Little Cap."

"The Bandits asked Trip to kill Little Cap!" I got very sick to my stomach.

"That's his mission," T-Bob said as easily as if he were saying that Trip was going to the store or making a snowman or something.

"When's it going down?" Doug asked.

"We got an ear inside the Rockies and we found out that they're moving Little Cap out of hiding during Reverend Walker's rally in the park. Everybody will be there and they figure the heat will be off in the hood."

"Where's Little Cap been hiding?" Doug asked T-Bob. "Where?"

"I don't know. It wasn't my thing, see? We just found out they moving him and only the people who gotta smoke him know info. They'll do it, too, no problem."

"Are you nuts!" I shouted. "Trip is all set on killing somebody and a little girl is stuck somewhere, hidden away from her mother and grandmother who love her and you're sitting here bragging! I do believe you have lost your cotton-picking mind!"

"You wanna slap the mess outta him, don't you?"

"Absolutely!"

"Now you see how I feel *every day,*" Doug said, and gave me an "I told you so" look. Then he turned to T-Bob. "Tell the lady thank you, T-Bob. She asked me to be cool so I'm going to tell everybody to treat you like china, even though you practically broke my nose."

T-Bob just dropped his eyes to the floor. "Could you loosen these cuffs? They hurt."

"Sorry, Bandit, it comes with the territory."

I opened the car door and got out. Doug followed and we both walked away from the squad car, out of sight of T-Bob.

"I see a light at the end of the tunnel, Georgia."

"Yeah, but I don't like what I'm seeing. Trip?! I can't believe it! All this time he was putting on! He didn't open that smart little mouth of his—that, that . . ."

"Little shit?"

"Yeah, I'm going to break his neck when I see him."

"That's the least of his worries. If he's going to try to take out Little Cap he's going to be toting some heavy firepower. And so will Little Cap and his posse. Trip is in big trouble."

"He could get killed."

"Exactly."

"What now, Doug?"

"Well, we have to find Trip. I'm sure he's somewhere getting ready for this evening. We've still got a couple of hours before the rally starts. If we can find out where Little Cap is then we can get him first, before Trip and his boys. We can't take a chance on them pulling out with Little Cap and the Bandits making a move on them. That puts too many people at risk."

"Can you get in touch with your informant in the Rockies?" He was a long shot but maybe he had some clue by now.

"It's tricky and I'm hesitant about stepping to him because he might not even know anything. He said he'd call. I've got an emergency pager number for him, but I've never used it before. I don't want to do anything that will blow his cover."

"Well, if there ever was an emergency, this is it."

Doug nodded. "You played the good cop to my bad cop very well."

"Doug, would you have beaten him?"

"Would you have let me?"

"I—I don't know."

"Good. It's nice to know that we're both human."

Then Doug turned to go and I reached out and hugged him. "Be careful."

"Georgia," he said, stroking my back with his hands. "You've got to trust that I can separate work from life. Just like I trust that you can, too."

I looked at Doug and saw a burning passion there—his own and mine as it reflected back to me in the steamy warmth of his eyes. I spoke from the heart. "Trust is what we've got to have in each other, to have a chance at any kind of a relationship, Doug."

Our hands touched and that spoke of the promise we both sensed was in the making. Then Doug walked away.

I wanted to go with him to track down the informant but I knew that hell would be a snow scene in a Christmas toy before Doug would let me tag along with him this time. Actually that was best. I needed to take stock of all that had happened and regroup. I would need to be at the top of my game for what was coming next: the rally. Little did I know that it would be the turning point in this baffling case.

TWENTY-TWO

The get-together spot for the rally was the parking lot of Sweeter Water Baptist Church. Zeke was there waiting for me just as we'd planned. He had his gear ready to go. We walked amongst the crowd, gathering background information that I would need to include in my story.

The building was originally the Cathedral of the Saints when the area was predominately white. After white flight, the parish fell on hard times. The Chicago Archdiocese decided to sell the church, which it did in 1978 to a group of neighborhood citizens armed with a King James version and a loan from a black bank.

They weren't just any group of neighborhood citizens, I was told. They all belonged to Sweet Water Baptist Church, a storefront, with a growing sanctified congregation. When they moved into the new building the members wanted to make a fresh start yet keep the original community feel of their church. They decided to call themselves Sweeter Water Baptist Church. The new name was suggested by Miss Mabel Stewart, who at the time was rocking Butter's mother in her carriage and petting her aunt Angel, who was playing on the floor.

Sweeter Water Baptist Church was a huge building, carved out of dolphin gray stone with narrow stained-glass windows. The two back doors were made of bleached wooden slats and had brass handles drilled in the center. The doors opened out like barn doors. A large crowd milled around.

What I saw was layers and layers of people who longed for change. Their expectations were high; they were just waiting to pitch a revival tent so they could celebrate how they got over this latest troubled time. It was a sad thing to see, a mass of people waiting for a miracle in the daylight of a society that cast shadows over miracles and the people who believed in them.

The response to this rally was bigger and better than many of us had anticipated—*us* being the media who collectively doubt just by the nature of the business. I once knew a reporter so cynical that if he had witnessed Jesus walking on water, he would have written a story about the prophet who couldn't swim.

Zeke was with the cameramen from all the other television stations. They shot b-roll of the signs that had been painted or drawn with markers on white boards and nailed to long Popsicle-thin sticks. My favorite two signs were: "Gangbanging done played out" and "If you can read this you're too smart to be in a gang."

I asked a couple of people about the Stewart family and they said Kelly was somewhere passing out ribbons and that Miss Mabel and the Olive Leaf Club were in the church basement. No one, they said, had seen Trip or his mother, Angel.

I eventually spotted Butter's mother, Kelly, handing out black and white ribbons. Kelly had her braids pulled back and tied up high in a ball on top of her head. Her hands clutched the ribbons as she twisted them together and knotted the ends, making a black and white pinstripe. She was working those ribbons.

Zeke was in close. He panned up from the box of ribbons, to Kelly's hands twisting them, to her face, also twisted with grief. Kelly saw us and smiled for a second then continued passing out the ribbons.

"Kelly," I asked easily, trying not to alarm her, "have you seen Trip?"

"No, I don't know where that boy is or my sister. They're both supposed to be here. Me and Mama just came on by ourselves."

I nodded. "Can I interview you about the rally?"

Kelly said sure, and I took a handheld mike from Zeke and started my interview: "Kelly, explain to us what the ribbons are for?"

"The black ribbon is in memory of Jackie." When she said the girl's name she had to choke back a sigh. "The white ribbon," she went on to say, "is in hope

215

for Butter's safe return. We're gonna wear 'em on our wrists."

"Do you think this march and rally will help convince the gang to return Butter?"

"Yes, I do. I don't know why, but I think everything is gonna be all right, I don't know why . . . but I just know," she said. I could see the faith in her eyes.

I wanted so much to tell Kelly what I knew about Trip hiding Butter. But now Trip was in danger of being killed or in danger of killing somebody. Telling her that would only shift worry from one child to another.

I wondered briefly if Doug had found his informant. What did he know? Where was Trip? I couldn't say anything to anyone. I quickly ended my interview with Kelly and let her tie a set of ribbons around my wrist.

Zeke and I headed inside the church looking for Miss Mabel. We walked down the marble stairs; we could hear voices humming and singing, no words, just a devotional hymn. The rhythm made me think of rivers washing against rocks, rain tapping against windows, hands patting against knees, feet stomping against floorboards, mouths talking in tongues, hips rocking against pews, and hallelujahs flying against ceilings.

"Sounds good," Zeke whispered in my ear.

That whisper moved me forward, down the stairs. All of the women were standing in a circle, including Miss Mabel and Auntie Vee. My grandmother could be one of their prayer posse. All of the women were dressed in white blouses and lengthy black skirts. They all had pressed, oiled, shimmering hair pulled away from their concentrating faces. They did not notice me or Zeke at first and we didn't want to be noticed. I heard the soft click of his camera and he wisely left off the overhead light and started shooting video of this engagement raw, just like it was.

Auntie Vee, no longer hunched over by grief on a hospital cafeteria table, was stouter and taller than I had realized. She was slapping her hand against a red-covered Bible.

Miss Mabel was clutching her black-covered Bible against her chest, popping up and down on her toes in sync with the clapping. Their voices died down and Miss Mabel began to pray. "Jesus, my savior in times of need. When I'se in trouble, where else can I go but to thee. Turn your eye from the sparrow and come by here, oh Lord, into the basement of our humble house of worship, Sweeter Water. Oh Lord, my God, our sorrows are running deep this evenin'."

"Yes! Yes!" Auntie Vee said.

I felt the ebbs and tides in her voice as Miss Mabel continued to pray.

"Lord, we want to ask you to bless Jackie's spirit this evening as we go about some important business in this neighborhood. The devil done got a toehold, a foothold, and a hip hold on things 'round here but we's here to say not for long—"

"How long, not long," a member of the circle said.

"We 'bout to get a prayin' spirit on these hood-

lums and my grandbaby Butter. We pray that you
wrap your arms around her and be a shield, send the
Holy Spirit to her wherever she is and wrap arms
'round Butter till the victory is won—and when it is
over, Sweet Jesus—bring Butter on back safe, happy,
and prayerful as she was ahfore and I know you will
'cause you a mighty God who answers prayers. These
blessings we ask in Jesus' name for our sakes, amen."

"Amen," said the members of the circle.

If that didn't fix everything, I thought, we're all
in trouble.

TWENTY-THREE

---

*M*omentum. March. Message.

The sun was low in the sky and had a beautiful glow to it when Reverend Walker began to speak. He shouted, his head back, launching the words into orbit, "What do we want?"

"Peace!" the marchers answered back.

"When do we want it?"

"Now!"

The marchers were walking six across, a good fifty rows deep. Across the front were Reverend Walker, Miss Mabel, Auntie Vee, Kelly, a man I recognized from the deacon huddle in the parking lot, and a woman I recognized from the basement prayer service. Zeke and I, like all the other television crews, had anchored ourselves to a spot well in front of the marchers to get a long shot of them walking toward us.

"Up with hope!" Reverend Walker shouted.

"Up with hope!" was the repeat.

"Down with gangs!" he said.

"Down with gangs!"

Zeke was lying flat on the street getting a tight shot of the ground as the army of feet came into the picture, and then he started panning up to focus on the faces of the people. Everyone in the neighborhood had agreed to move their cars from the street so the marchers would have a clear path to the park. A hazy, golden shadow was cast back and away as the marchers walked past us. They had spaced themselves just right so that their shadows were falling back and adding another layer to their ranks. Somebody, somewhere had done some stone-to-the-bone, black-power fist-in-the-air protesting back in the sixties. This rally had that kind of a feel to it.

"What do we want?" Reverend Walker shouted.

Bang! Bang! Bang! Bang! came the response to his words. I jerked around in time to see the crowd hit the street in waves, like a tide rolling out. Zeke was on the ground, his camera still on, still rolling. I quickly got down on the ground next to him. I looked up and around at the houses and the two flats on the street. Then I saw little shards of paper floating down from the sky.

"Awww, wasn't nothing but firecrackers!" someone yelled. Then we heard a loud rattling sound. Three little boys were laughing from behind a couple of garbage cans. I recognized them immediately as the little boys I'd given the ice cream to. One of the marchers spotted them and yelled, "Hey, there they are!"

The boys took off running down the closest alley.

Slowly everyone began getting up, Zeke first. I was waiting for my heart to stop pounding. He took his camera off his shoulder and laughed.

"Hey, gimme a hand up!"

"Naw, I'm already overworked as it is!" Zeke said, ignoring me.

I slapped at his pants leg until he reached down and pulled me up.

The marchers were shaking off the commotion: some mumbling, others cursing, all disjointed. Then Reverend Walker started it up again: "What do we want?"

"No firecrackers!" someone answered in a playful voice.

Everyone laughed, including Reverend Walker. "I say, What do we want?"

"Peace!" the crowd shouted and they began marching again.

There was a squad car stationed at every other corner. I looked around for Doug. I didn't see him anywhere.

We finally reached the park, the field house being the stopping point. A plywood podium had been built right next to the field house, nestled against the park swimming pool. There were folding chairs for the preacher and politicians lined up in two angles that faced the oncoming crowd. The marchers spread out in front of the podium.

I got ready for a long, long sermon by Reverend

Walker and more speeches from other political power mouths. Zeke began milling through the crowd, picking and choosing his shots to conserve precious power in the battery pack.

Suddenly I felt a hand on my shoulder and a voice in my ear. "Where your cop friend at?"

I turned to face Angel, Trip's mother. She looked worse than the last time I had seen her, if that was at all possible. Her skin was splotchy, her face was drained of color, and her hands were shaking. She was rocking nervously. Angel still had on the T-shirt Butter had won at the spelling bee. She asked again about Doug.

"I don't know where he is. Are you okay?"

"You don't know?!" She groaned. "Damn, when you need a cop you can't find him!"

"Angel, it's okay—"

"No!! No!! How the hell is it okay? Huh?"

"Angel, let's just get one of the officers around here—"

"Naw, naw, that ain't gonna work. I want him. He know Trip and he would fix it with the law!" Angel said, and put her hands in front of her face.

She was coming loose at the seams. Tell her what I knew? In her shape? I had no choice really.

"Oooh-we," Angel said, rocking. "I got the jitters!"

"Where's Trip? Angel, we gotta find Trip because—"

"I know! I know! I know what Trip's done and what he tryin' to do. I know!"

"You know that Trip hid Butter?"

"Yeassssss!"

222

"All this time you knew!" I shouted at her.

"Hell no! Do you think I'm crazy or something? I just found out," Angel said, standing in front of me rocking and scratching her arms. "I didn't know before he done hid her! If I'd ah knowed that I'd ah whupped his ass and made him tell it. But now Trip 'bout to get in more serious trouble. One of my friends told me, wanted to cop some of my hit and I said naw and she—she said I know somethin' you wished you knowed. And then she said it's 'bout Trip and what he did and gonna do. She told it all. I knew she wasn't lying 'cause she sleeping with one of the top ones in the Bandits and I know she wanted them drugs badder than me. She wanted 'em badder than me."

"Angel, let me just tell one of these officers and I know—"

"No! Can't trust 'em! I'll go myself!" Angel turned and slid around the side of the field house. I ran after her. We were hidden by the building as we walked across the open grassy area of the park.

"I was with Detective Eckart when he arrested T-Bob. He's out now trying to find out where the hit is going down."

Angel looked exhausted and weak, her steps shaky. I took her by the arm and said, "Let's call the police—"

"No!" she said, looking wild-eyed, then she clutched her head. "No time. It's happening now. I know—know where. Y'all think I'm bad, but I'm not. I'm not bad! I gived up almost all of my stash to find out 'bout Trip, to save him. Ain't that love?"

"Yeah, Angel," I said softly. "I know you love Trip. Tell me where? Huh? Just tell me where and we can get the police and fix it?"

"No-no-no!" Angel moaned, and she shook her head.

"Why?!"

"I ain't stupid! You done fo'got? They go in shootin' not askin' no questions. What they care about shootin' some little black boy who gets in the way? I gotta go get him myself now!" She started to jog the rest of the way across the field.

I couldn't let her go alone, could I?

TWENTY-FOUR

Angel moved quickly down the streets and alleys, every other step giving me a glimpse of the heels of her slip-and-slide shoes. We finally reached the back stairs of an abandoned building. The fingers of her right hand trembled as she clutched the corner and peered around the brick wall. She motioned for me to follow her, pointing with her finger. Two doors down I could see a young man rocking against a fence, smoking a joint.

"Top floor is where Little Cap is at. He'll be down any second now."

"You sure?"

Angel nodded and I noticed that her entire body was shaking.

"Are you okay?"

She nodded yes when the answer was clearly no.

I silently cursed myself. Why hadn't I flagged down a cop?

Angel peeped around the corner again. "See?!" she whispered, and pulled her head back. I saw three guys walking down the back steps, looking cautious but not as guarded as I thought they would be. They wore the yellowish-gold colors of the Rockies. I noticed one, a dark-skinned young man with a long ugly scar on his face. I recognized him from the mug shot that I had seen at the cop shop and from the picture in his mother's house. It was Little Cap.

My eyes darted around, looking for Trip. Where was he?

Angel was nearly sitting on the ground, her body racked with spasms. She turned her head and spit up.

"You're too sick to move, Angel."

The three Rockies were walking toward the alley now.

"You gimme some money when this over?" she begged. "You gimme some money to buy me some stuff?"

I heard a car door slam. Where was Trip?

"Okay, okay," I lied, trying to calm her down. I didn't want her voice to carry.

I heard another car door slam. Where was Trip?

"You go stop Trip now, huh? Can't—ca—can't hard—ly move. I needed all my stuff. Ain't have none to give away. Trip done messed me up." Angel moaned as she held her sides and rocked against the building. "Go on! Go on!"

I didn't know what to do. Instinct pushed me

forward, down the rear walkway. I was looking around wildly, trying to spot Trip. I heard a car engine crank up. By the sound I could tell it was an old car. Just as I reached the fence at the end of the yard, the car grunted past. It was a late model long Caddy with a torn black vinyl top and a gurgling muffler. The car eased down the alley. I opened the gate and stepped out, watching the car pull away. Just as it neared the end of the alley, two shopping carts filled with tin cans came rolling out, blocking the exit.

The car began to slow down.

I took two steps forward, then stopped, not sure what was actually happening or what I should do.

The car stopped with a lurch about forty feet away from me. Although my mind was shouting warnings at me, I couldn't see anyone. I was looking all around for some sign of Trip.

One of the shopping carts fell over and the cans started rolling out into the street and into the alley. The car doors opened. Little Cap stayed in the backseat. The driver and the other gangbanger got out.

Just as the two guards stood up and out of the way of the car doors I saw two teenage Bandits, black bandannas covering the lower half of their faces, come out from behind garbage cans in the rear, guns drawn. They opened fire.

I ducked behind a thick electrical pole and my heart jackknifed into the pit of my stomach. I peered out from behind the pole and saw the Rockies on the ground. I heard one of the Bandits yell for Little Cap to get out of the car. He moved out slowly. I couldn't hear that much of what was said because I was so far away.

Then I saw him. Trip had a black bandanna over his face as he stepped out from behind one of the garages. He had a gun in his hand and he was shaking. They left Little Cap for him to kill.

"Trip!" I yelled. "Don't!"

He turned and looked my way. It was then that Little Cap made his move. He spun, pulled out his gun, side-stepping toward cover while firing off two shots. One hit the Bandit standing nearest the car's trunk, dropping him with a splatter of blood where he stood. As he hit the ground, his mouth became a raw socket prickling and sizzling dangerous sounds. The other shot just missed Trip, who dived for cover.

Seeing Little Cap this close showed me the raw power that he had. He was tight, his movements mechanical as he decided when and where to strike next. Suddenly, I heard, "Trip! Trip!" Angel was yelling and staggering down the alley. "Trip! Trip!" she called.

Little Cap fired.

The shot struck her in the chest. I heard the resisting crunch and thunk of bone and flesh.

"Mama!" Trip yelled, dropped his gun, and began running toward her.

The Bandit with Trip yelped, "No!"

Little Cap whirled and fired at the boy who tried to warn Trip; the bullet tore at his chest and laid him out flat on his back, blood gurgling from a jagged tear in his upper body.

I ran forward. I saw Little Cap now aiming at

Trip's back. I lunged and felt my body make contact with Trip. I felt as if I were floating. The pictures and sounds that whirled around me smothered my ears and erased my memory because I forgot everything except how to breathe.

I hit the ground and I felt my flesh tearing away from my arm. I felt Trip's body beneath me and my momentum made us roll over and over until we hit something hard. Whatever it was stopped our movement. I heard Trip crying and I thought about how much I hated what was happening and then I heard footsteps running toward me. He's coming! I thought. Seconds became drips of a lifetime.

I struggled to get up, to fight with my bare hands for myself and for Trip. I looked up. I saw Little Cap fire over his shoulder before hopping a fence as the police began entering the alley. My heart was encouraged when I spotted Doug headed my way. He reached me, his gun low at his side, "Georgia? You okay?"

I shook my head and all the anger, and adrenaline, and hate that had been building up inside of me escaped through tears that I felt no shame in shedding.

"Mama!" Trip mumbled, crawling away from me over to Angel.

"An ambulance is on the way," I heard someone say. "Damn, that Little Cap must be part rabbit—see him take that fence? But don't worry, he can't get far. We got this place covered like flies on shit." And for the first time I noticed the other officers beginning to swarm through the alley.

Trip was hugging his mother and I saw a big red splotch of blood covering the T-shirt she had on. I looked at Doug as if to ask him whether or not Angel was going to make it. He hunched his shoulders.

I felt blood running down my arm. "Oh Doug, I'm bleeding."

"Easy, Georgia, let me see," Doug said, gently taking my arm. He picked up the black bandanna that had covered Trip's face and gently tied it tight around my upper arm. Then Doug took out a handkerchief and dabbed at the wound. "Just a bad cut, not to worry, you'll be fine."

Doug helped me up and hugged me close to him as we walked together over to Trip, who was huddled around his mother's shoulders. His lips moved slowly, awkwardly, as if he were reading to her from a primer about the violence that had become the story of their lives. I stared at them until the glint of flashing lights stole my attention away from Trip and his mother. Three cops were moving the shopping carts and kicking cans out of the way so paramedics could make it down the alley with a stretcher.

"Hold on, Mama," Trip told her. "Hold on!"

I hoped that she heard him.

I eased Trip away from his mother. I held him close, my palms across his chest, rocking with the sporadic movement of his breathing while the paramedics worked to stabilize Angel and get her on the stretcher.

Trip reached out as they began to wheel her down the alley. "I'm going!" He jerked away from me and tried to run until Doug caught him and asked, "Where's Butter?"

Trip wiped away tears and said, "She in the basement in our secret playhouse in the crawl space."

Doug called to one of the officers and told him to drive Trip to the hospital. We watched as they put Angel into the ambulance and Trip into a squad car. When they pulled off, Doug said to me, "Let's go."

All the time she was there. In the Stewart house. Butter had managed to hide under our very feet. When we got to the house it was locked, but Doug jimmied the back door open, and I started calling as soon as I stepped inside. "Butter! Butter!"

"Sssh!" Doug said. "You'll scare her!"

But I couldn't stop. I just kept calling as I went through the kitchen. "Butter!" I didn't call in anger. I didn't call in frustration. I just called. "Butter!"

I opened the basement door near the sink and Doug and I walked down the stairs. It was cool in the dusty and unfinished basement. The concrete floor was shellacked black by dirt. Old furniture was stacked up in every corner. Water from a leaky pipe dripped down from one corner of the room, staining the wall rusty red. I looked around and I saw a square door that was only waist high. I cracked it.

"Butter!" I called. "Baby, it's okay."

We heard a bump and I spread the door all the way open and looked inside.

There was Butter, wiping the sleep from her

eyes. She was lying on a pallet of blankets. A flashlight with its head wrapped up in newspaper was in the corner giving off hazy light. A plate and a cup were pushed into one corner. I saw a half-eaten bag of potato chips and two ice cream sticks pushed off in the corner next to a stack of children's books.

Butter's eyes were wide with fear as she doubled her knees up against her chest. There was enough room for her to sit up comfortably and just enough space for me to lean in and say, "Butter, remember me? The TV lady? You can come out now, honey. It's all over."

Butter shook her head no.

"Butter, honey. See this man behind me?" And I moved away slowly to show her Doug, who gave Butter his officer's friendly smile.

"He's a good policeman. Trip told us where you were. He said it was okay for us to come get you."

She looked almost convinced but was still hesitant.

"Baby, I wouldn't lie to you. How else would we know where to come? You and Trip are such good hiders, plus I'm the one who bought you the Eskimo bars."

Butter smiled and moved toward me. I pulled her out of that dirty, dark hole and hugged her. Doug patted her on the back as she laid her head on my shoulder.

"C'mon, kiddo, you wanna go outside in the fresh air and sunshine?"

"Yeah," Butter said softly.

"How about to the park?"

"Oooh, yeah!"

"Good," I told her as I began walking up the steps. "That's good because your mama and grandma and a whole bunch of other folks are there just dying to see you."

TWENTY-FIVE

They'll just have to wait," a voice from above me said.

When I heard that voice, the muscles in my legs froze. The muscles in my neck did not. I jerked my head up and stared, stunned.

Butter buried her face in my neck and began to cry.

Doug was standing behind me, right angled, and I saw him reach for his gun.

"I'll blaze your ass, man," Little Cap warned.

Little Cap was standing in front of us in the doorway, looking down with the orange glow of the remaining day behind him. He looked like a henchman from hell waiting to do some low-down dirty deed. I heard his mother's voice in my head: "God, is that really my child?" and I shivered.

Butter looked up at me and already her face was beginning to splotch red from her sobbing.

Little Cap looked tired; he was hurt and his gun hand was shaking.

"H—h—how?" I semi-stuttered.

"I got away. Made it these few blocks and then I spotted you from the gangway across the street," he huffed, saliva dripping from the right corner of his mouth. "Y'all left the door open."

Doug spoke up. "Don't try this, man. All the police in this area are out, and all of them are out looking for you. You don't have a chance."

"With them two I do, homey."

Butter buried her face back in my neck and wailed.

"Shut up!"

Doug stepped over to the railing that bordered the stairs leading down into the basement. Little Cap aimed at his heart.

"Listen, man," Doug said. "Leave them alone. They'll slow you down. Take me."

"What? I look like a fool, man? You'll try to pull something 'cause cops always think they Batman. You always played Batman when you was a kid I'll bet? Caped Crusader and other bullshit, betcha, huh?"

"Look at them," Doug reasoned. "The kid will be crying the whole time and she'll be moving like a snail trying to carry her."

"Naw, I'm taking them. They're safe passage. Now," Little Cap said, gun still shaking slightly. "Drop your gun, easy, with one finger."

Doug did exactly as he was told. He reached for his sidearm with a crooked index finger. Butter cried louder, the muffled sound vibrating against my skin. I heard Doug's gun clatter against the concrete floor. I took a step up on the stairs. They felt unsteady beneath my feet.

"Keep coming," Little Cap hissed.

I took another step. Butter was getting so heavy.

"Don't move, man, until they clear," Little Cap told Doug.

I reached the doorway and Little Cap stood back next to the refrigerator. I walked by the stove and heard Doug walking up the steps behind me. Little Cap was standing off to the side, three feet away at an angle where he could watch both Doug and me.

I could hear the wind blowing outside and Butter was sniffling in my ear, all cried out but getting heavier and heavier by the second.

Doug reached the doorway, hands held high, spread wide.

"Easy, man, easy . . ." Little Cap said, his eyes narrowing.

Then the wind kicked up and the back door rocked back, making a loud creaking sound that made Butter jerk. My knee gave way. Little Cap turned toward the door, then back. That's when Doug lunged for Little Cap's hand, throwing his arm up toward the ceiling and forcing the gun to fire. Shards of glass came raining down on us. The bullet had hit an overhead light.

I swung my body around and Butter's foot

caught a grease can on the stove, flinging it out in the direction of Little Cap and Doug who were fighting over the gun. The cold, slick liquid soaked their hands, making Little Cap's gun squirt out of his grip.

I set Butter down and pushed her into the farthest corner. "Get down!" I shouted. I dropped to a crouch by the stove.

The gun hit the floor, firing again, this time tearing a plug out of the wall. I knelt down. Doug slammed his fist into Little Cap's ribs. The gun was spinning like a top. I got on my knees and reached for the gun with outstretched hands.

A roundhouse punch by Little Cap landed in Doug's side, forcing him to drop to one knee in pain. Little Cap lunged for the gun on the floor. Doug tackled him around the legs.

I grabbed the gun's handle and it slipped away, the grease coating my fingertips.

Little Cap's hands landed on top of the counter.

I reached for the gun again.

Little Cap reached for a butcher knife.

I shoved the gun with my hands toward Doug.

Little Cap grabbed the knife and glared at me with hatred as he pulled his arm back, aiming for my heart.

Doug fired off two quick shots, hitting Little Cap. I saw death in the eyes that had planned death for me. I prayed that Little Cap wouldn't fall on me and God answers prayers because he fell back and away, against the refrigerator.

I stretched out both my hands and Doug grabbed them, pulling me to him. I let myself fall forward without fear. It was all over except for the shouting.

The only light in the room came from the strawberry-scented candles, each one blazing intently, fresh and new like our relationship.

The only sound in the room came from our short breaths, anxiously awaiting this first deeply intimate sexual encounter.

The only hesitation in the room was in our minds, not our hearts—for after all our yearning, we could only hope our fantasy of each other together would live up to reality.

Doug lay next to me, his shirt stripped from his back, a soggy ball tossed at the foot of the bed. He used two fingers to slowly slide first one, then the other spaghetti strap away from my shoulders before pulling my entire tank top down to expose my breasts. Their new-found freedom was short-lived. Doug took them prisoner again with his hands and with his mouth.

We were at Doug's place, three nights after Butter's case was solved. It's a cute little house with bay windows and bookshelves in every room—including the bedroom. This seemed odd at first, until I noticed all the titles were on having a healthy sex life or on erotica.

Boyfriend is something else.

We tested some of the theories out on his bed that first night. And other nights. Doug is probably the only man secure enough in his masculinity to have a canopy bed. Said his ex-wife bought their first one and he has loved them ever since.

I wonder, is it the bed or is it just us?

Our sexual appetite is unquenchable. And when we touch there is a singular feeling of belonging. Passionate and consuming kisses behind ears, on nipples, on bellies, over each other's heart. . . .

I must say that I love me some him.

I think it's been easier for us because Doug and I haven't locked horns or hooked up together again on another story-slash-case.

But I know in my heart that we can get through it when it does come our way again.

Isn't faith a beautiful thing?

STORY SLUG: BUTTER UPDATE
REPORTER: GEORGIA BARNETT
10PM SHOW NOVEMBER 28
THANKSGIVING!

(***PACKAGE***)

VIDEO (TRIP FALLING INTO PILE OF
LEAVES, BUTTER HOLDING RAKE)

"Whee!"
"I'm tellin', Trip! You not
helping!"
(**REPORTER TRACK**)

CHYRON LOCATION: SOUTH SIDE

TRIP AND BUTTER ARE RAKING
LEAVES IN THEIR NEW FRONT
YARD. THEIR FAMILY MOVED
HERE LAST MONTH AFTER A
BLACK BUSINESSMAN OFFERED
TO HELP THEM FIND A NEW
HOME.

MISSING CHILD POSTER

BUTTER, YOU MAY RECALL, WAS
MISSING FOR SEVERAL DAYS
THIS SUMMER AFTER SHE
DESCRIBED A GANG MEMBER
CHYRON: LAST AUGUST/FILE DRIVE-BY   WHO WAS THE TRIGGERMAN IN
CRIME SCENE   A DRIVE-BY SHOOTING.
(***STOP/SOT***)

CHYRON: LAST AUGUST/BUTTER
JOHNSON

"I seent a car. This real dark
black boy with a scar, he was
dressed all in yellow, and just
shooting his gun!"
(**REPORTER TRACK CONT**)

MUG SHOT OF LITTLE CAP

BUTTER DESCRIBED THIS MAN,
ALEXANDER DARRINGTON,
KNOWN AS LITTLE CAP. HE WAS

240

A MEMBER OF THE ROCKIES STREET GANG AND WENT INTO HIDING.

WALKING SHOT UP TO HIDING SPACE IN BASEMENT

AFRAID FOR BUTTER'S LIFE, TRIP HID HIS COUSIN INSIDE THIS STORAGE SPACE IN THEIR BASEMENT. HE GAVE HER FOOD, INCLUDING POPSICLES. (***STOP/SOT***)

CHYRON: TRIP STEWART/10 YEARS OLD

"I knew I had to do something. I told her to stay there and be quiet. It'd be okay. I'd do anything to keep them from hurting Butter." (**REPORTER TRACK CONT**)

FILE/ALLEY WHERE HIT WENT DOWN

ANYTHING MEANT AGREEING TO HELP KILL LITTLE CAP AS PART OF THE INITIATION INTO A RIVAL GANG, THE BANDITS. LITTLE CAP AND THREE OTHER GANG MEMBERS DIED THAT DAY.

PARAMEDICS WORKING ON ANGEL

BUT TRIP'S MOTHER, ANGEL, STOPPED HIM FROM FIRING A SHOT—AND IN THE PROCESS TOOK A BULLET FOR HER SON. SHE RECOVERED.

PAN SHOT STEWART FAMILY AT THANKSGIVING TABLE

ANGEL IS NOW ENROLLED IN A DRUG REHAB PROGRAM. SHE WAS ALLOWED TO COME HOME FOR THANKSGIVING. (***STOP/SOT***)

CHYRON: MABEL STEWART/BUTTER'S
GRANDMOTHER

"We have a lot to be thankful
for. The children are okay,
Angel is trying to get back on
track, and we got a new house
and a chance to be safe and
happy."
(**REPORTER TRACK CONT**)

DISSOLVE TO SHOT OF FAMILY HOLDING
HANDS, PRAYING

A CHANCE THAT THE STEWART
FAMILY IS THANKING GOD FOR
THIS HOLIDAY.
GEORGIA BARNETT,
CHANNEL 8 NEWS.

END OF PACKAGE/TIME: 2:45 SECS

SIMON & SCHUSTER HARDCOVER
PROUDLY PRESENTS

HIT TIME

YOLANDA JOE
Writing as ARDELLA GARLAND

Available February 2002
from
Simon & Schuster Hardcover

Turn the page for a preview of
HIT TIME. . . .

Story Slug-Cold Charity
5 P.M. Show, December 3rd

.......ANCHOR INTRO.......
(DAN READS)

CLOSE-UP

The American Heart Association is telling the
Elite Swim Club to go jump in the lake.

Literally.

Once again it's time for the club's annual
charity event, the Winter Relay. Club members
have collected $10,000 in pledges this year.

WJIV's Georgia Barnett is live at the
lakefront with details.

Georgia?

(*********STOP*********)

TAKE LIVE SHOT
CHYRON LOCATION: LIVE/MANNING PIER
LIVE/GEORGIA BARNETT/CHANNEL 8 NEWS

.......(GEORGIA LIVE).......

Dan, we are having unseasonably warm weather for December. Today's high was around 50 degrees. But that'll do very little to knock the chill off the ice-cold waters of Lake Michigan.

The race is now in its tenth year. A swimmer will start at the pier, go out to that buoy and back, then the next swimmer will take off.

As you can see behind me, I'm surrounded by family and friends of the Elite Swim Club. They're here to cheer on their loved ones for charity.

.......(NATURAL SOUND/
CROWD CHEERS).......

The swimmers are lined up. The official is ready to start.

.......(CROWD COUNTS DOWN/
STARTER PISTOL SHOT).......

And they're off! Wow, look at them go!

.......(NATURAL SOUND RACE/
WIDE SHOT).......

Now if you, the Channel 8 audience, would like to help the Elite Swim Club reach its goal by making a donation call the number on the bottom of your screen....

.......(PANDEMONIUM IN WATER/
WIDE SHOT).......

Something's . . . something's wrong . . . I can't tell . . . the swimmers are coming back. They're panicking!

.......(VARIOUS SWIMMERS
SHOUTING).......

Oh my God! Help! There's a body! It's a man! A dead body in the lake! Oh my God!

* * *

WHAT A TRIPPED-OUT WAY TO START A WORKWEEK.

Monday afternoon I went out to do a live shot about a charity event, a simple feel-good story—an *easy-pleasy* I call it. That *easy-pleasy* turned ugly-wugly right there during my live shot with three hundred thousand viewers watching.

Eyeballing the ugly.

We stayed hot with the coverage. I was live. When the police arrived—when they pulled the body out of the water. My ace cameraman, Zeke Rouster, was all over the video, getting shots of the scene from various angles. I was hustling. I was giving detailed descriptions about every little thing that was going on. I sounded like a sportscaster except my play-by-play involved divers, detectives, and dead men.

Dead men tell no tales.

Or answer any questions either for that matter.

Like . . . who was this man? Was this an accident? A suicide? Or could it be murder?

It's like a TV game show, except there's no Regis and no grand prize. The viewers follow the story intently as it unfolds, waiting for the right answers, wondering how it'll all turn out. And it's a hard game to play too except for the people who must . . . like the police and the press.

In this case that would be my boyfriend Doug and me. Who knows how many twists and turns this news story will take before winding down to the truth. Who knows?

LIKE A FISH OUT OF WATER, I WATCHED THIS DEAD body sag in the hands of those who hauled it out of Lake Michigan. The deceased had on black pants, a red-and-black-checkered jacket with big, flap pockets. In those pockets were bricks soaked clean from being in the water.

Had this man figured that he could weigh himself down with a few bricks, hoping that their weight and the weight of his desire for death would be enough to sink him?

If the dude was going for suicide, he rang the bell and won the prize.

If a killer was trying to hide the deed, the mark was badly missed.

This body had found its way near shore. The *who* and the *how* of it was a puzzle for cops and journalists to figure out. I was struck by the man's hands: green, next to frigid blue, next to bruised red. Without question I was eyeballing the combination quilt work of death and water. The damage those two bad boys can do together on the human flesh is more than a notion.

And this stiff wasn't a young cat either; he had

gray hair, cut close, and brown age spots speckled his thick neck and sloping chin. His white skin was stained a sickly yellow. The skin, that's the first thing that takes a major hit when you die. The skin. Gives up the ghost like it ain't nothing. Turning flat. Stiff. Hardly showing signs that there was ever any life at all.

My favorite cameraman, Zeke Rouster, was standing behind me getting a pan shot from the victim's head to his toes. Zeke then did a squat and grunted so loud I almost laughed. His jelly stomach went from three months pregnant to six; a sistah wouldha cracked on him if the situation wasn't so doggone grave.

One of the detectives rolled the victim on his side and water sloshed out of his ear. Zeke was a film fiend, panning and zooming, catching close-ups and cutaway shots of the club members still huddled together in awe of the tragedy playing out before them.

"It's not pretty is it, Zeke?"

"Never is, Georgia," he said, flipping on the camera's overhead light. Zeke grunted again as he stood up, then took a swing at a stubborn section of white hair that kept falling into his face. "I'm getting too old for this shit."

"Not a chance, Zeke. Old cameramen never retire, they just fade to black. You're still the best shooter in town."

"Edit text. You mean the planet."

Zeke is about as modest as a nude baby on a bear rug. He loves to be stroked. I don't mind stroking him either, because he deserves it. Zeke is a news cowboy ready to go anywhere and do whatever it takes to get the story right. He has paid a stack of dues too over his many years and always has my back. Like now . . .

"Yo, Georgia," Zeke said, giving me one of his mischievous green-eyed winks, "here comes Detective Love Jones!"

Zeke was a teasing somebody. I didn't want to smile but, doggone it, I did. Before I even looked up, I knew Zeke was talking about Detective Doug Eckart. Obviously he'd caught this case. We hadn't worked the same incident since a little girl named Butter disappeared in late summer. On that case we initially bumped heads, then put our heads together, and eventually our hearts.

Doug glanced in my direction but played it cool. We didn't want our business in the street. The top cops Doug needed to impress to move up the ranks might not like our relationship, and my rival colleagues might cry foul thinking I'm gleaning inside info between the sheets.

"Clear that camera back," Doug said to the police support crew. "This is a crime scene, not a movie."

Zeke sarcastically sucked his teeth.

"Suck 'em any harder and you'll need braces!" Doug barked.

The cops all laughed.

Zeke rolled his eyes at Doug. Then he hunched his shoulders at me as if to say, *Get your boy in check.*

But I had no issue with Doug. It was mandatory that he take charge. And he wasn't hurting us a smidgen. We'd already done three live updates. We were also assured the lead story spot at six.

"Don't fret," I said lightly patting Zeke's back. "We're beating everybody on this story."

I moved to get an interview with Erin, one of the swimmers who had dived in and made the grisly discovery. Erin was badly shaken up, so much so that after she got out of the water her voice vanished.

Speechless and trembling like a dry leaf, Erin was comforted by her friends. I made sure the paramedic gave her a good looking-over. Now Erin stood off to the side with a grave marker on her shoulders—face stony, eyes hard, lips engraved in a frown.

"Erin, we're about to go live, can you please just give us a minute?" It took several seconds for what I'd said to register. Girlfriend was shaken up for real! It'd be more than a minute before Erin would feel good about sleeping with the lights off again. Her electric bill would be mighty high.

"Yes, sure, I can talk . . . a little." Erin forced the corners of her mouth to turn up ever so slightly. Then she ran a nervous hand over her shiny brown hair, slick with lake water.

Zeke set up behind me, balanced the camera on his knees, framed the shot up, giving her depth, adding more intensity to her words.

"Turn your body left." Zeke made two back-handed swipes with his hand. "Good. That's perfect."

We got set for a live update. The director cued me in my earpiece and I was on. I gave a quick intro recapping the charity event that led to the grisly discovery. Then I did TV news like it should be done. I let Erin tell the story just as she'd experienced it—up close and personal.

*   *   *

"I was in the water, you know? It stung, the coldness of it. I was a championship diver in college, so I know how to get control of my body under water. I went a bit deep, then I began to float up. I pulled away from the rest of the swimmers. As I got closer to the buoy, that's when I saw it . . ."

Like metal to a magnet, Erin's fingertips were drawn to her lips. She gulped twice before continuing her story.

"I looked and there he . . . was . . . this man . . . his hair floating like seaweed or something, helpless-looking, arms out, dead as can be."

"Erin, can you remember your first reaction and what you were thinking at that moment?"

"I screamed and swallowed a little bit of water. It took every fiber of my being to stay calm. I kept thinking, I gotta get out of this water, back to shore, get help. Then everyone was yelling. It was chaotic. I can't tell you how upsetting . . . how—how . . ."

Then Erin began to cry. I gently put my arm around her shoulder and closed off my live shot.

"The police are here on the scene trying to determine if this is an accident, a suicide, or a homicide. Right now it is classified as a death investigation. The identity of the victim remains a mystery. We will update the story as more information becomes available. Georgia Barnett, live at Manning Pier. Back to you in the newsroom."

*　*　*

Out of the corner of my eye I saw Doug examining the body. The boy has skills. A few times Doug has talked to me about some of his old cases. Intent and deliberate, he had explained to me how the investigations went—how something minute captured his attention and just wouldn't let go. Those kinds of things were always the prologue to the case, Doug told me. The beginning. The beginning that started you on the path to the end.

I worked on my long story, or package as we call it, adding more interviews from the swim club members.

I also interviewed Doug. By then other television reporters were there, some scowling and others smiling, giving me my props, not for catching a story that fell right into my lap, as it most certainly had, but for knowing how to run and score with that bad boy once I had it.

Doug was keeper of the info. All of the reporters surrounded him, a gang-bang as we call it in the business. The questions hit him rapidly. Doug deflected and dodged those questions like a championship boxer, only unleashing powerful tips when he was ready. I let my colleagues lead.

"Whatcha got, Detective Eckart?"

"A short time ago this case changed from a death investigation to a murder investigation."

"You ruled out an accident or suicide pretty quickly."

"Well, it's pretty hard to shoot yourself in the back."

"Multiple gunshot wounds?"

"Two shots."

Then I began asking more pointed questions as I stood in the crowd, thinking, remembering what the dead man looked like fresh out of the water. The front of the torso remained clean, besides, of course, the water damage. There were no exit wounds in the front.

"Detective," I asked, "were the shots fired from a great distance or from a small-caliber gun? There were no exit wounds on the body."

Doug's eyes smiled. *Yeah, baby, you've been listening to me and the boys chatter.*

"The weapon in this case appears to be a small-caliber. Yes."

"Was this a robbery?"

"That is a possible motive. The victim did not have a wallet or anything containing identification on his body."

So it was very likely a robbery. But why go to all the trouble of moving the body? This pier is pretty secluded in the winter, so whoever brought the body down to Manning Pier had a good chance of not being seen. True. But why would a regular old stickup ace do that?

Doug began giving a description of the victim—white male, sixty to sixty-five years old, five nine, muscular build, 170 pounds, gray hair, brown eyes, wearing a red-and-black jacket, black pants and shoes—all before wrapping up the gang-bang.

"Right now the investigation is moving forward, the body is in the capable hands of the coroner. As we get new information that we can pass on to you, we will do so."

That was cop slang for, *Get out my face now 'cause I got work to do.*

We gave Detective Ace some space. Reporting crime stories is easy in the beginning. Clues are few. There's not a lot to sift through yet. Every reporter there—from NBC, ABC, WGN, and FOX on down—ended their live shots the same. And that was with a physical description of the victim and a plea to the public for help; if anyone thought they knew the victim or if they'd seen something strange in the area around Manning Pier, they should call the police.

I waited for Zeke to give me a ride back to WJIV after our last live shot. Usually I tried to grab a cab or drive my own car if I could instead of hanging around until Zeke finished meticulously packing up all the equipment.

But I was in no rush tonight. You see, Doug and I had an after-work date, but by now our after-work plans were out of whack. We both had expected a light workday. We both got our heads bumped by reality.

I was truly an unhappy sister. Had tickets to the Symphony Center to see the dynamic diva Leontyne Price. Now our work was jamming us up like a fender-bender during rush hour. Don't you just hate it when a funky workday interferes with your personal life?

So Doug and I ended up skipping dinner and the performance. Instead we would hook up late and kick back at my twin sister's place, the Blues Box.

Visit
❖ **Pocket Books** ❖
online at

---

www.SimonSays.com

Keep up on the latest new
releases from your favorite
authors, as well as author
appearances, news, chats,
special offers and more.

SIMON & SCHUSTER
A VIACOM COMPANY
www.SimonSays.com

Pocket
Books

2381-01